I0628224

Webb's Wondrous Tales
Book 4

Webb's Wondrous Tales
Book 4

Mack H. Webb, Jr.
Illustrations by Celia Webb

Pilinut Press, Inc.

Webb's Wondrous Tales
Book 4

Copyright 2019, Mack H. Webb, Jr. and Celia Webb

All rights reserved.
No part of this book may be reproduced, stored in a retrieval system or transmitted by any means, electronic, mechanical, photocopying, recording, or otherwise, without written permission from the author.

Book and cover design by Celia Webb

Pilinut Press, Inc.
Warrenton, Virginia
www.pilinutpress.com

The Pilinut is the edible seed of the *Canarium ovatum* tree which is native to Southeast Asia. Tasting like sweet almonds, it is eaten for its health benefits including prevention of anemia and for nourishment of the brain and nervous system.

Library of Congress Control Number: 2019903090

ISBN: 978-1-944390-03-7

Table of Contents

Cluck, Cluck, Goose

oday a pall hangs over Cinagro farm. The reason for this is because during the night a chicken disappeared from the hen house. It is one of many that have vanished over the past weeks. Speculation has it that a fox is the culprit. But no one on the farm, man or animal, can say with certainty.

Each fowl on the farm is nervous, and watchful, lest they be the next to be taken. So absorbed are they with their plight, they hardly notice when a stray goose shows up at the farm.

The goose arrives waddling on tired webbed feet. It has been forced to make its way on foot, ever since its close encounter with the business end of a hunter's shotgun. The goose survived the encounter, but sustained an injured wing that prevents flight.

The goose's inability to fly has made it an outcast from the gaggle of geese it used to live with. So it has roamed from one place to another, seeking a home and friendship. It does not look promising that the goose will find either on Cinagro farm.

1

It isn't that the barnyard animals are hostile towards the goose. On the contrary, in the week that the goose is on the farm, the other animals do not even acknowledge its presence. The goose may as well be invisible.

Only the farmer has been kind to the grounded goose. He provides shelter and makes sure the goose gets its share of food and drink.

The goose is grateful for the farmer's generosity, and wishes there was some way to express its gratitude. The goose gets its chance late one night, when a fox with an empty sack sneaks into the farmyard.

The fox is bent on stuffing a fat chicken into the sack. Slinking into the hen house, the fox nabs a sleeping hen and puts it into the sack before it can cry out. The fox then creeps from the coop without disturbing the other snoozing chickens. The fox is already salivating at the thought of the chicken dinner to come.

"HONK!"

The fox whirls with alacrity at the dreadful sound, dropping the sack in the process.

Presented with an escape route, the chicken flutters from the sack and to safety within the barn.

The fox is about to give chase when the goose says, "Mr. Fox, please let the hen go. Take me instead."

All animals share a universal language, so the fox understands what the goose is saying. After sizing up the plump, juicy goose, the fox agrees.

"Alright," says the fox, opening the sack. "In you go."

"There is no need for me to get into that musty sack," says the goose. "I'll walk beside you."

"Suit yourself," returns the fox.

It is quite a distance to the fox's den, and along the way the fox has time to consider the situation. He grows suspicious. "Hey goose," says the fox. "Why do you give yourself up so easily?"

"Because I want to be your dinner, that is why," replies the goose. In reality he is willing to forfeit the remainder of his days to save the farmer's chicken, as payment for the farmer's kindness.

"Hmph!" snorts the fox. They travel the rest of the way to his den in silence.

Once inside his den, the fox blocks the entrance with a large stone. "Yahaa!" exclaims the fox, licking its chops. "Dinner time."

"Yes," says the goose, "I suppose it is. How will you have me? Baked? Fried? Roasted? Broiled? Fricasseed?"

"Huh?" asks the fox, somewhat perplexed.

"If I were you," says the goose, "I'd bake me."

"W-what?" stammers the fox.

"Where do you keep your baking pans?" asks the goose, as he explores the den.

"I..." says the fox.

"Never mind," says the goose, "I have found them." He chooses the largest pan. He steps into the pan and lies down.

"What are you doing?" asks the fox nervously.

"Making sure I fit," replies the goose.

"Something is very wrong with this goose," mutters the fox to himself. "And there would have to be something very wrong with me before I'd eat it!" The fox inches towards the entrance.

When the goose is satisfied that the pan is the right size, it begins to pluck its feathers.

When the fox sees the goose removing its own feathers in preparation for being baked, the fox's nerves snap. He hurriedly rolls the stone from the entrance and bolts from the den. The fox pours on even more speed when the goose emerges from the den yelling, "Come back, Mr. Fox!"

The fox is quickly lost from view. The goose sighs and goes back to the farmyard.

A hero's welcome greets the goose. None of the animals shall ever forget that the goose sacrificed itself for one of their farmyard companions. Henceforth the goose lives like a king, getting the best feed and the cleanest water.

The goose receives all of this gladly, happy to be surrounded by friends in a place that it can call home.≡

Cluck, Cluck, Goose

Finny the Fish

This is Finny. Finny, like most fish of the sea, spends most of his day in school. Finny doesn't learn much though, his mind is always on other things. Today is no exception. Finny should be paying attention to his professor, who, chalk in hand, stands before a small blackboard. On the blackboard is a drawing of a row boat. Inside the boat is a stick figure of a man holding a pole with a line and hook. Yes, Finny should be paying very close attention to this lesson. Instead, he is daydreaming of walking along a sandy beach while dressed in a fine suit of clothes.

Finny wants more than anything else, to live on land. He is tired of the watery home he has known for so long. He has heard tales of other types of fish that have made their home on land. The mudskipper, lungfish, and the Northern Snakehead fish can choose between water or land as it pleases them. Finny knows he can do it too, and he has a foolproof plan.

Finny practices every day at holding water in his gills. He plans to have a big adventure on land, and certainly doesn't want to aerate to death.

As time goes by Finny is able to hold his water for a considerable amount of time. At last he feels he is ready to make his first real test on the land. Late one night, he wriggles to the edge of the surf and onto the beach.

At first all he can do is flip and flop about, but soon he manages to balance himself on his tail. Then, shifting his weight from side to side, he finds that he can make forward progress. He can hardly contain his excitement. After several nocturnal practice sessions, Finny is ready for his big adventure.

Two days later, Finny dons a disguise consisting of a pair of colorful Bermuda shorts and a hat made of kelp. So dressed, he heads into town.

Finny is a few yards from town when a flock of birds become interested in him. Finny is so alarmed that he almost loses his water. Beaks and taloned-feet swoop ever closer as Finny does his best to escape with his scales intact.

Of a sudden, Finny feels something close tightly around him. Poor Finny is being clutched by the pudgy hands of a child. This looks like the end of Finny. But Finny is slick and slippery. He manages to wriggle free. He flees; eluding the child by ducking into an alley.

Finny's luck is short lived however, for he has stumbled into an alley where hungry cats dwell. The felines are rummaging through trash cans in search of sustenance. Finny sees the green-eyed, long-fanged cats at the same time as the cats see Finny. Finny bolts from the trash-strewn alley with all the speed his fins can muster. Trash cans and trash fly in every direction as an army of slavering cats spring from the trash cans and give chase.

What a sorry fix poor, wretched Finny is swimming in. Surely he is done for. "Fins don't fail me now," Finny silently pleads. Finny runs with all of his might to the water and its sanctuary, hampered only slightly by his drooping Bermuda shorts. As he nears the water, children and birds join the pack of cats in the chase. Hands, bird feet, and cat paws earnestly endeavor to clasp fins with Finny.

A cat's claw clips Finny's tail causing Finny to lose his shorts and kelp hat. Finny's eyes are large as he glances back toward the chaos. Finny thinks his world is going mad, and for him, indeed it is. He makes a desperate lunge for the sea. At that same moment a huge wave comes crashing down.

Finny narrowly escapes, leaving in his wake the children, cats, and birds sprawled and drenched from the wave of sea water. One of the sodden cats wears Finny's shorts on its tail. Finny's kelp hat sits askew on a drenched bird, a souvenir from the fish that got away.

As he darts to deeper water, Finny is unable to recall why he ever wanted to leave such a wonderful place as the sea.≡

Finny the Fish

The Fox

(Inspired by "The Fox and the Grapes", an Æsop (Sixth century B.C.) Fable)

O ne day a fox is roaming the countryside when a great thirst visits him. Search where he might, water is not to be found. There are no trees to afford him shade and the sun's heat is relentless.

After a time the fox happens upon a vineyard. He stretches out in the shade of the vines and pants heavily. The ripe grapes dangling from the vines are just the things to rehydrate his parched throat. However, even when he stands on the tips of his hind paws the grapes are still just beyond his reach. The fact that he is unable to acquire the grapes makes the fox even thirstier than before. Unlike the fox in another story you may have read, this fox is more resourceful.

Not to be out done, the fox puts sticks one on top of the other. The pile is soon sufficiently high and the fox mounts the pile. He is just about to bite into an enticing bunch of grapes, when the vineyard owner appears.

The fox turns to look at the vineyard owner, a rotund man with a terrible grin on his face. In the man's right hand is stout tree limb. In his left hand are two leather leashes that tether two pathetic dogs.

The fox, keeping his eyes on the man and dogs, steps carefully backward from the pile. Once on solid ground the fox flees from the vineyard with all of the speed his legs will generate.

"Get after that fox, you curs!" bellows the man to his dogs. He releases their leashes and when the dogs are reluctant chase the fox, the man lays into them with the tree branch. The flogging propels the dogs, barking and growling menacingly, after the fox.

The dogs give it their all. However, even though nearly dehydrated, the fox easily outruns them. The dogs are only a few hundred yards into the chase and they must stop to catch their breath. All they can do is whine, whimper, and watch the receding tail of the fox. Their master will not be pleased.

The fox halts some yards away. He turns to assess his pursuers and finds them quivering and heaving like bellows. The fox can tell by the dogs' bone structure that they should be magnificent beasts, but instead they are useless skin and bone. No doubt their condition is a result of rough treatment from the vineyard owner. It is a sad state of affairs, but the fox can do nothing about it...Or can he?

Eventually the fox finds water and he drinks until his belly sags. Not long afterwards, he comes across an area in a wood where wild grapes grow. Remembering the vineyard and the delectable grapes that escaped his pallet, the fox tries a bunch of the wild grapes. The fox finds them utterly delicious. As he chews cluster after juicy cluster, the fox gets an idea.

He travels deep into the woods until he comes to a vast clearing. In the clearing the fox digs several rows of holes. When that is done, he goes to where he knows cattle are being pastured.

At the pasture the fox hails the head-of-the-herd. "Good-day to you, Mr. Bull," says the fox to the bovine. Although most humans would not understand the exchange of words, it is well known that animals share a common language. "Good-day," snorts the bull. "Is there something you want here?"

"Why yes there is," replies the fox. "I would like to take some manure from your pasture."

The bull is surprised by the request, but says, "Help yourself. There is plenty more where that came from."

The fox is delighted. He gets a large, leaf-covered tree branch and piles manure onto it. The manure laden branch is dragged to the clearing; its load is dumped into one of the pre-dug holes, and mixed with soil. The fox continues this process until all of the holes are amended with manure. Next the fox retraces his steps to where the wild grapes grow.

The fox eyes the unruly tangle of vines and contemplates. He then chooses a fairly stout vine and begins to chew it through. It is very rough going and the fox's jaws are soon tired and sore. "There must be an easier way to cut through this vine," the fox muses. He hunts along the forest floor until he finds what he is looking for, a sharp-edged stone. With the sharp stone held firmly in his mouth the fox quickly cuts through the vine. When he has severed as many vines as he desires, he digs them up, takes them to the clearing, and plants them in the prepared holes.

The labors of gardening have given the fox a powerful appetite. After a few moments of stalking through the woods, he has a couple of quail to fill the void in his stomach. As he lay quietly digesting his meal, he remembers the thin-flanked dogs and imagines the beating they must have received for their failure. The fox decides to pay the dogs a visit.

It is an easy matter for the fox to locate the dogs, and one look at them confirms his suspicions. The dogs have indeed been chastised by the vineyard owner. The fox would not have thought it possible, but they look more starved and pitiful than when he had first seen them. The fox approaches the prostrate dogs, for he has come bearing gifts. He drops a quail before the muzzle of each dog.

The dogs are too weak and bruised to raise a paw, so they can only whimper their thanks.

The fox retreats to the forest, but returns daily with gifts of fowl or fish.

The dogs become strong and healthy. The relationship between them and the fox is one of friendship. One day the dogs chew through their tethers and, leaving their wicked owner behind, follow the fox into the forest where they make their home.

The seasoned vines in the clearing grow vigorously and the next year they are loaded with purple-black bunches of grapes. Upon tasting the ripe fruits, the fox immediately notices that the grapes are exceptionally flavorful and sweet. They are far superior to the untended wild grapes in the forest. The fox is pleased and smacks his lips with satisfaction. The fox's ruminations are interrupted by the two dogs.

The dogs and the fox have been constant companions for the past year. Now the dogs, high with excitement, come to the fox with news of something they have found in the forest. The fox and the dogs move swiftly and silently through the forest until the fox sees what has excited the dogs.

A man-child, a girl the age of twelve to be exact, is curled-up and sleeping on the moss of the forest floor. Her dress is soiled and ragged and her dirty face is streaked from her tears.

The fox concludes the girl is in almost as bad a condition as the two dogs had been. He also concludes she too must have had a cruel master. The fox knows what must be done. He goes foraging in the forest and returns just as the girl is waking up.

The girl awakens slowly for she is weak and hungry. However, when she catches sight of the fox and dogs staring at her in the tree-filtered sunlight, she jumps to her feet. Suddenly she feels lightheaded and collapses to the ground where she lies bewildered and frightened.

The fox approaches the girl slowly, lays a quail beside her, and retreats a distance to sit by the two dogs. This simple act of kindness will ensure the girl's survival.

The girl has never known kindness, so cannot recognize the fox's gesture as such. But she senses friendliness in the fox and dogs, and she is certain they mean her no harm. The girl is not without skills, or else she would have left this world long ago. The prospect of eating fuels her recovery.

After starting a fire with two sticks and some moss, she quickly dresses the quail using a sharp stone. In short order the quail is sizzling on a spit, and soon after that, consumed with relish. When she has finished her meal, she thanks her hosts which have remained seated a polite distance away. "Thank you, Sir Fox and Sir Dogs. My name is Giselle. I don't know what would have become of me if you had not happened along."

The four live together companionably in the forest-clearing. The dogs and the fox help drag wood and materials to the edge of the clearing, and using it, Giselle constructs a dwelling. Her first attempt is not very sturdy and a wind gust topples the home. More than once Giselle's construct collapses, but she perseveres. Over time and after several modifications, she ends up with a fine, well-built abode. Giselle is happy and more content than she has ever been. The dark memories of her past life are fast fading.

One day the vineyard owner who mistreated the dogs, notices smoke rising from within the forest. He travels through the forest until he comes to the clearing where the fox, dogs, and Giselle live. First to catch his eyes are the rows and rows of well-tended grapevines. They are laden with beautiful grape clusters. The vineyard owner feels a pang of jealousy. He does not recognize the type of grape, but he does recognize competition. "There is room for only one vineyard in this valley," he fumes to himself, "and it is mine!"

Next to catch his eyes are the little house and the smoke rising from a cook-fire. "I will have a word with the owner of that house," says the vineyard owner. Moving towards the house he calls out, "Anyone home?" And, although it is not true, he continues with, "I come as a friend!" No one answers.

Unknown to the vineyard owner, Giselle had spotted him before he had reached the clearing. She recognized him immediately and began to quake all over with fright.

The fox, sensing her fear, nudged Giselle toward the trees where she now sits out of sight.

The fox remembers the vineyard owner too, as do the dogs which round on their former master barking and posturing menacingly.

The irate dogs terrify the vineyard owner. He does not recognize his former charges, for when they were in his possession; the dogs were never seen in such a high state of health. The dogs harry their former master for some distance through the forest, ensuring that he will not visit the little clearing again for a long time.

The fox, knowing something about the ways of man, decides the vineyard owner could still make trouble and disrupt their tranquility. He quickly devises a plan. The fox takes a large basket Giselle has fashioned from grapevine prunings and fills it with bunches of grapes. Holding the handle of the now heavy basket in his mouth, the fox beckons Giselle to follow him. They stroll through the forest until they come to the edge of a bustling town.

Animals can easily communicate with humans when they wish, and so it is that the fox quickly conveys to Giselle why he has brought her to the town. Giselle is to go into the town and sell the grapes that are in the basket.

Giselle is apprehensive about venturing into the town. She knows first hand how wicked humans can be, having spent time in, and run away from an awful orphanage. Giselle does not know that all orphanages are not bad places; she has only her one experience to draw upon. Also there was her encounter with the vineyard owner when, tired and hungry from her trek away from the orphanage, she had sampled a bunch of his grapes. The vineyard owner discovered her and, using a stout stick, had thrashed Giselle from his vineyard. However, despite her misgivings, Giselle has faith in the fox's wisdom and so does as he bids.

Giselle gets her first customer after being in the town only a minute or two. The customer, upon sampling his purchased grapes, touts their deliciousness loudly and at great length. Other customers gather around Giselle and quickly buy every grape she has to offer. Before Giselle is allowed to leave, she is asked to promise to return the next day with more of her exquisite grapes. She makes and keeps the promise.

Since that day many seasons have passed and many changes have occurred. An enormous amount of money has been made, and continues to be made, by selling grapes in nearby and distant towns. At the behest of the fox, Giselle used a portion of the money to buy the land on which the grapevines in the clearing are growing, and thousands of acres besides.

A lovely home has been built for Giselle, and very fine dog houses for the dogs. The fox prefers the out-of-doors as his home.

There are many more grapevines in the clearing, and they are now tended by workers formerly employed by the wicked vineyard owner. They enjoy working for Giselle, whom they deem a kind and gentle employer.

When the wicked vineyard owner falls on hard times because no one desires his inferior grapes, Giselle purchases his property cheaply. Rather then let him live out his life in poverty, Giselle, the fox, and the dogs forgive him.

The former vineyard owner lives happily with the four, and atones for his misdeeds as best he can until an illness lays him to rest. Every year at the anniversary of his passing the fox, Giselle, and the dogs lay flowers at the former vineyard owner's final resting place, for through him four lives have been changed forever. He had been malicious for most of his life, but in his last days there was goodness found in him.

Giselle has grown to be a very beautiful young lady. She has a wealthy young man from a nearby town courting her.

The fox in his wisdom knows that it will not be long before the two are wed and living in happiness. He decides it is time to resume his life in the forest. He has been too long living among mankind. It is also high time he sought a mate for himself and raised a family. The fox bids farewell to Giselle and the dogs, but communicates to Giselle that someday he will return for a visit. And so he does, with a female fox and five kits in tow.≡

The Fox

The Greatest Magician in the World

The Great Omeleté is a magician. He travels around from town to town peddling his magic act. Some day he hopes to make it big on the magic circuit. This is highly unlikely, for during every one of his acts he is booed and hissed by the audience. Various rotten fruits and vegetables are hurled at him, and the Great Omeleté usually ends up with egg on his face. Despite the bad reviews, he perseveres.

It is late at night, and the Great Omeleté is gathering his belongings from the sidewalk. It is where they were thrown along with the Great Omeleté, when another of his magic acts turned sour.

There is nothing left for him to do but begin the trek of 25 miles that will see him to the next town and better prospects. He is cold and hungry. These are not new sensations for him; he has been cold and hungry before. As a matter of fact, he cannot recall a time when he has not been cold and hungry.

He is several miles along the road when it begins to rain. It is a heavy stinging rain that sends him looking for shelter. He finds shelter in the form of an old ramshackle house.

Were the weather not so foul, the Great Omeleté would think twice or even thrice before entering the teetering structure. However, the weather is foul, so he plunges in and promptly falls through the rotted floorboards.

The Great Omeleté lands on the packed-earth floor of the basement. He lays stunned for a moment, and then he flexes his limbs to satisfy himself that nothing is broken. He is in pain, but is otherwise okay. Rising to his feet, he coaxes a flame from his pocket lighter and surveys his surroundings. There is no way to the upper floor, but there are stairs leading further downward.

He weighs his options. Wait where he is and hope help arrives, or follow the stairs in the hope they lead to freedom. He opts for the stairs. Holding his lighter high over his head, the Great Omeleté begins his descent.

Cobwebs are thick within the passage, and red-eyed rodents chatter at him as he passes. The Great Omeleté does not like this place, and will be glad when he is free of it.

The stairway continues ever deeper into the bowels of the earth. The pocket lighter flickers and goes out. Darkness and dread engulf the Great Omeleté.

He has lost track of how long he has been in the musty passage. And he is beginning to regret his decision to descend the stairs, when he hears voices. The voices are faint, but resonate. He increases his pace for he can see the glow of light ahead.

When he finally reaches the bottom of the stairs, he steps into a vast chamber. The chamber is so large, that despite the bright light within, the ceiling is lost in gloom.

In the middle of the chamber is a large circle in the pattern of a wagon wheel. Seated at the end of each spoke is a magician. The magicians number ten, and they are engaged in a singsong chant. They cease abruptly when the Great Omeleté enters the chamber. All of them rise and their eyes bore into their intruder.

"Uh…" says the Great Omeleté. "Sorry for barging in like this, but if you would be so kind as to…"

"It is HE!" bellows one of the magicians, while pointing a finger at the Great Omeleté. "He has arrived, just as it is written in the ancient text. He is the one of great power who will lead us in our bid to take over the world!"

"T-take over the world?" stammers the Great Omeleté. "Now hold on a minute!"

"How can you be sure that he is the one for whom we have waited centuries?" asks another magician.

"Yes, we must have proof." says yet another of the magicians. "Let us have a demonstration of his power."

"A demonstration?" says the Great Omeleté. "Now you're talking my language." He walks to the middle of the circle and opens his box of magic tricks.

The circle of magicians leans forward anticipating the great spectacle to come.

With a grand flourish, the Great Omeleté pulls a colorful bouquet of flowers from his sleeve.

The circle of magicians are speechless. This is certainly not what they had expected. One of the magicians executes a grand flourish, and the chamber is filled with a lush tropical forest. Another flourish and the chamber is back to normal.

The Great Omeleté clears his throat. He produces a coin, and using slight-of-hand makes the coin disappear. He walks over to a magician and retrieves the coin from behind the magician's ear.

The magician yawns. With a wave of his hand he conjures up a massive mound of gold coins.

The Great Omeleté, stupefied, gapes at the gold. He struggles to compose himself. He twists his ear, and a hen's egg pops out of his mouth.

One of the magicians turns himself into a griffin and lays an egg. From the egg emerges a miniature griffin, which flies about the chamber. A moment later, all is back to normal.

The Great Omeleté blows out a breath and swallows hard. He smiles weakly, picks up his top hat, and pulls from it a white rabbit.

A magician removes his cap and reaching into it, pulls out a gigantic fire-breathing dragon. The dragon roars and portions of the ceiling crash to the floor. A moment later the dragon is gone, but the scent of brimstone lingers.

The Great Omeleté is pale, his mouth is dry, and he could really use a restroom right now.

The circle of magicians is greatly agitated. They are unimpressed by the Great Omeleté's feeble attempts at magic. It is time they did away with him.

The Great Omeleté, sensing ire rising in the magicians, holds his hands out for silence. From his box of tricks he retrieves a cloak and cap. He puts them on. Now he looks like a proper magician.

The circle of magicians leans forward.

The Great Omeleté has one more trick up his sleeve, a real showstopper meant for a grand and special occasion. He decides there will never be a better time to use it than now.

He closes his eyes and begins to mumble a chant. Soon sweat is glistening upon his brow. He grows hot, and hotter still, until he fears he might ignite into flames.

Just when the circle of magicians begins to grow impatient, the room shimmers with a silver-flecked brilliance. The chamber vibrates with raw energy.

Never has the circle of magicians felt such a force. For the first time in their existence, the ancient magicians know fear. In a last desperate act they rush the Great Omeleté, but it is too late.

There is a deafening "SNAP", as might be heard could a lightning bolt be broken in two. And in that instant, the circle of magicians vanish. All that is left to show they ever existed are ten putrid pools of smoking slime.

Totally exhausted, the Great Omeleté slumps to his knees and gulps air. He is awestruck by what he has managed to do.

When he has sufficiently recovered, he dumps the magic tricks from his box. After what has happened tonight, he can never be satisfied with mere parlor tricks. He fills his empty box with as much gold as he can carry, and then searches for a way to the surface. He finds one. It is another stairway.

After a tedious climb, the Great Omeleté opens a door to the outside world. He stands for a moment breathing in fresh air and letting the rain wash over him.

He will give up practicing magic and try hard to forget what took place below. He hoists his box of gold and trudges into the rainy night. As he does so, he cannot help but reflect on this night's performance. Tonight he had given his finest performance and there is none left to bear witness to his feat.

The Great Omeleté is the greatest magician in the world, but no one will ever know.≡

King for a Day

*J*ulius is sitting on concrete steps in front of his house; drumming his fingers and idly watching dark clouds gather overhead. The converging clouds are not very interesting, not like the spectacular meteor shower which took place last night. Now that was something to see!

Julius blows out an impatient breath before checking his wristwatch. Of a sudden, he leaps to his feet and thrusts wide the door to his house. "Mom!" he hollers. "Are they done yet?"

"For the tenth time, Julius," says his mother, "no."

"Aww, Mom," pines Julius, "can't they cook any faster?"

His mother gives him an exasperated look and sighs.

Julius is hungry. He is not hungry for just any food; he is hungry for French fries. The mere thought of French fries makes him want to turn cartwheels of happiness. For Julius, there is nothing better than the aroma and taste of a steaming-hot French fry.

Finally the fries are ready and his mother dumps a heap of them into a brown paper bag and hands the bag to Julius.

Julius accepts the oil-spotted bag and hugs it to his chest, "Thanks, Mom." He exits the house and strolls through the neighborhood while savoring his fries.

Julius is well into his feast when he holds up one of his French fries and examines it closely. It amazes him that a simple slice of potato can delight him so. He is jubilant and moved to celebrate its tastiness with a rhyme.

"French fries fresh, French fries hot,

You think I'll share, but I will not.

French fries so good, they make me sing,

I wish I were a French Fry King!"

POOF!

No sooner has Julius finished his rhyme than he begins to feel quite strange, and very unlike himself. It isn't until he sees his reflection in a shop window that the full extent of what has happened rocks him. Julius has been turned into a giant crinkle-cut French fry with arms and legs. To be more exact, he is a French Fry King complete with a crown and scepter. "OH NO!" he wails. "Oh no!" he wails again, for a boisterous bevy of blackbirds has converged upon him and now peck at his crispy exterior.

Julius tries to ward them off by flailing his scepter, but the birds are not deterred. Julius flees. The birds, squawking and chirping happily, flap after him. As he runs he heats up and emits an appetizing aroma of freshly cooked French fries. This delights the birds and they redouble their efforts. It is only when Julius strews the contents of his bag that the birds relinquish their chase, opting for the smaller crinkle-cut versions of the crown-wearing Julius. Julius, tossing his empty bag into a trashcan, trots on.

A rumble of thunder heralds the release of moisture in the form of cold, fat droplets. The birds, morsels held firmly in their beaks, quickly disperse in search of shelter.

Julius too searches for shelter, lest his crispy exterior becomes sodden. He finds sanctuary in the form of a large, plastic playground tunnel. He crawls in and, physically and mentally exhausted by the recent events, drifts to sleep. An hour later, cold water swirling about his bottom awakens him. He groans.

Within the darkened 10-foot long tunnel, the fragrance of French fry pervades. The odor, previously a catalyst for unbridled glee, causes tears to well up in Julius' eyes. He is fearful that he shall forever resemble a crinkle-cut. However, a bright flash of lightning reveals the truth.

During the brief flash of light, Julius sees that he has been transformed to his former figure. Full of relief and happiness he abandons the tunnel and races home through the sheeting rain.

"Oh, Julius!" says his mother when he enters the house. "You're soaked to the skin!"

"Mom!" begins Julius. "I was just turned into a French Fry King! I was all golden brown and crispy, and I had a crown and a scepter! And these birds they--"

"Oh, Julius!" says his mother disapprovingly. "You have such an imagination. Get cleaned up and into dry clothing this instant. Dinner is almost ready."

"But, Mom!" pleads Julius.

"Right now, Julius," returns his mother.

Julius turns to do as his mother bids. While en route, the aroma of French fries reaches his nostrils. His skin prickles. He rushes to a mirror and is relieved to see his normal reflection. Julius looks into the kitchen and espies a large plate of fries on a counter. He glances over his shoulder before slipping the fries into a trash can. He cannot bear the thought of eating a French fry, not after having been one himself.

The next day Julius and his family are out shopping and they stop for lunch at a hot dog stand. While they wait in line to make their orders, Julius scans the patrons seated at tables surrounding the stand. His eyes come to rest on a little girl and her parents as they apply condiments to their hot dogs.

The little girl, after squeezing out ketchup and mustard, claps her hands in merriment and declares, "Hot dogs are my absolute favorite food!"

Julius grins openly at the girl's remark, but his smile fades when the girl begins to sing.

"Ooohh I wish I were an Oscar M--."

The girl is not far into her jingle, when Julius intervenes. He dives onto her tabletop scattering plates, hot dogs, and condiments. He finally comes to rest with his right hand clamped firmly over the little girl's mouth. She and her parents stare at Julius in wide-eyed surprise, but Julius' eyes are wider as he earnestly pleads, "Don't say it! Don't even think it! Get it out of your head!"

Julius' mother and father animate themselves and haul Julius from the tabletop, all the while apologizing for their son's uncustomary behavior.

"Julius, how could you do such a thing?" admonishes his mother. "What has gotten into you?"

"Mom!" says Julius. "That girl was about to--."

"Young man," interrupts Julius' father, "we'll talk about this later. When we get home you will go straight to your room."

"But, Dad..." bleats Julius. And seeing that it is useless to try to explain, he slumps into a dejected silence. Julius is led away. He glances back and winces at the scene of the girl and her parents trying to remove ketchup, pickle-relish, and mustard from their clothes, faces, and hair.

The girl has lost her appetite and whines to be taken home.

At home she cleans up properly and then goes outside to play. She has almost reached the playground when she begins to sing and hum her favorite melody. "Ooohh I wish I were an hmm-hmm-hmm-hmm wiener." POOF!

Meanwhile, Julius is sulking in his bedroom. As he sulks, he takes a moment to reflect on his time as a French Fry King. "Maybe I imagined the whole thing," he says to himself. And then he says with astonishment, "Or maybe not!" This sudden change of opinion comes as he gazes through the room's window. He is just in time to see a giant hot dog in a bun zooming by and easily out distancing a boisterous bevy of blackbirds.≡

The King of Beasts

a lion's roar rips through the savanna. It causes birds and beasts to scatter in terror and dread. The King of Beasts has this effect on his subjects and with good reason. An up-close encounter with their ill-tempered monarch could spell disaster.

No animal dares question the lion's right to rule, although the lion has not always reigned as the King of Beasts. Ages ago, before human beings roamed the earth, the elephant reigned as the King of Beasts. This is a fact Merlin the mandrill knows all too well.

Merlin the mandrill is an ancient simian. He has acquired an unparalleled knowledge of the magical arts and he possesses the wisdom of the ages. Merlin dwells in a hollow tree that has stood on the savanna for millennia. He is within his dwelling teaching his apprentice, when he hears the lion's roar. "Listen to that wretched lion making all of that racket," says Merlin to his apprentice. "King of beasts? Bah! No king should govern his subjects by tooth and claw."

"But that is the way it has always been," says the apprentice.

"No, young one," says Merlin, "it is not the way it has always been. Come, it is time you knew the truth." Merlin leads his apprentice to a large bowl of water. Into the water he squeezes a few drops of juice from a wizened root. He then stirs the water with a stick while mouthing a chant.

"Look upon the mystic water," says Merlin. "Gaze deeply and you shall see and hear the events that took place during the reign of King Pachydermo, the last of the elephant kings."

The apprentice gapes with wide eyes and slack jaw as the water swirls cloudily. Slowly the water clears, and the apprentice views and hears the figure of King Pachydermo.

King Pachydermo wears a plain circlet of gold upon his head as a sign of his kingship. The elephant king raises his massive trunk high above his head. He emits a trumpet that vibrates across the landscape. Birds and beasts halt what they are doing and turn toward the sound. Another trumpeting follows closely behind the first.

Moments later, beasts of every size and shape emerge from the surrounding growth and assemble themselves before the majestic bull-elephant.

Every animal is rank and file with its like kind, and the total number is somewhere in the millions. The din of their chatter quiets down, and they all look expectantly at their king.

There has never, before or since, been an elephant to rival the sheer bulk of this imperial beast. To compare Jumbo to King Pachydermo would be like comparing an infant to that giant among men, Goliath.

King Pachydermo's eyes wander over his subjects for a long moment before he says, "There are those among you who have chosen to ignore the laws I have set for governing my realm."

Silence reigns.

The king fixes his eyes on Carnivroe, the leader among the lions. "Carnivroe, come forward," commands King Pachydermo.

Carnivroe, a majestic figure in his own right, steps forward.

"It has reached my ears that you and your pride are not content to hunt only for food. You must hunt for sport as well. For the sheer joy of it! With my own eyes I have seen your unfortunate victims, stretched out and drying in the sun. How is it that you, Carnivroe, my trusted second-in-command, could do such a thing? That you would do this beneath my very trunk is unforgivable. As ruler of this realm, I will not tolerate such unwarranted acts of slaughter. Carnivroe, what have you to say for yourself? Speak!"

Carnivroe remains silent.

"Since you choose to remain silent," says King Pachydermo, "I hereby banish you and your pride from this realm. Be gone by sundown and never return."

Carnivroe eyes King Pachydermo and quakes with rage upon hearing the decree. His muscles tense, and for a brief moment he contemplates springing upon the massive bull elephant.

King Pachydermo senses Carnivroe's intentions. Even so, he stands as unmoving as a mountain.

The moment passes, and Carnivroe edges slowly backward submissively. He knows he is no match for his former monarch.

Animals part left and right which allows the outcast Carnivroe and his pride an avenue of departure.

A full year passes, during which the exiled lions obey the ruling passed by the elephant king. Now, however, they have a mind to get revenge against their former sovereign.

Carnivroe pays a visit to Merlin the mandrill.

"I have been expecting you, Carnivroe," says Merlin, as Carnivroe enters Merlin's sanctum.

Carnivroe is taken aback for a moment. How, he wonders, could the old simian have foreseen his coming? Carnivroe resolves to finish his business and leave the mandrill's dwelling as quickly as possible. Recovering he says, "Then you must know why I am here."

"Yes," says Merlin, "I know why you have come. I also know what my fate will be, should I decline to give you what you require."

"You are indeed a wise simian," says Carnivroe with a grin that displays a great number of his finger-long teeth.

"Take this gourd," says Merlin, as he hefts a gourd the size of an ostrich egg. "Sprinkle its contents onto the water in the elephants' sacred watering hole."

"I sincerely hope your spell is satisfactory, Mandrill," says Carnivroe quietly with narrowing eyes, "or I shall be back for your hide." Carnivroe picks up the gourd and heads for the elephants' sacred watering hole.

The sun is almost on the horizon by the time Carnivroe reaches the watering hole. From an overhang he dumps the gourd's powdery contents onto the water. The powder causes the water to turn purple and blue, before becoming crystal-clear. Carnivroe smiles wickedly and settles himself low on the overhang to await the elephants.

It isn't long before the elephants arrive in a shuffling mass at their watering hole. King Pachydermo has the honor of being the first to drink. He hesitates, sensing something strange in the otherwise normal-appearing water. With his trunk he probes just above the water's surface.

Carnivroe, watching the scene from above, suddenly fears that he may be discovered. He begins to formulate an escape plan. He won't need it, however.

After taking an experimental sip, King Pachydermo finds the water to be cool and sweet. He drinks deeply. All of the other elephants follow suit.

Of a sudden, the elephants begin to reel, as their consciousness spins dizzy. King Pachydermo looks up and catches sight of Carnivroe smirking down at him.

The sight of Carnivroe outrages the king. Immediately he knows the lion is in some way responsible for what is happening. "You dare defy my decree?" bellows the Elephant King. "I will have your mane for this!" King Pachydermo charges the cliff face, ramming it with his monolithic forehead. The landscape quakes beneath the blow, and Carnivroe topples from his perch to land at the king's splayed feet.

The monarch encircles the dazed lion with his trunk. He raises it aloft and then begins the swift descent that will put an end to the treacherous Carnivroe. The king sounds a great trumpet-like roar that causes Carnivroe to mewl for his life.

Suddenly the full power of the magic powder finally engulfs the king. He hesitates. His foe-laden trunk stops in mid-descent.

King Pachydermo blinks twice in rapid succession, trying to remember what he was just about to do. He cannot recall. His mind is void of every memory. He releases the lion, unable to remember why he had it in the first place.

Carnivroe is perplexed, but grateful for his release. He runs and does not stop until he is again with his pride.

Days pass and word spreads that King Pachydermo remembers nothing of his past. The daylong he wanders aimlessly on the savanna, with all of the other elephants in tow.

Finally the news reaches Carnivroe's ears. He musters his courage and ventures into King Pachydermo's realm to see for himself if there is any truth to the rumor. What he finds is a herd of elephants, King Pachydermo in their midst, milling about the savanna. "It is true!" says Carnivroe gleefully.

Carnivroe is quick to establish himself as self-appointed King of Beasts. It is the beginning of a new era.

Merlin and his apprentice watch as the vision in the water bowl fades and then disappears.

The apprentice's eyes are still wide and his jaw is still slack. He looks at Merlin in disbelief. "You?" says the apprentice. "It was you that dethroned the elephant king? How can that be? It happened eons ago."

"I am older than you could ever imagine," says Merlin. "I did not myself dethrone the elephant king. Yet, it is true I had a part in it, and for that I am ashamed. However, the effects of the powder shall not last forever. Even though generation upon generation have come and gone, the day when the elephants shall remember their past is at hand."

What Merlin says is true. Even now a group of elephants has come across a circlet of gold. The circlet is the golden crown worn by the extinct King Pachydermo. The elephants probe the crown with their trunks, and a spark of memories gone rekindles in their minds. It is the beginning of a new era.≡

Mocking Bird Blues

eep! Beep! Beep! Beep! Beep!

Yvonne reaches over to her alarm clock, turns off the offending timepiece, and through blurry eyes reads 4:45am. Yvonne groans. She would love to sleep for just ten minutes more, but knows if she does she will be late for work.

Yvonne drags her protesting body from beneath warm, comfortable sheets and starts another day. This day will be just like the ones before.

After washing-up, brushing her teeth, dressing, eating breakfast, and sitting for hours in a jam of traffic, Yvonne will arrive at work where she will attend meetings all day.

In the meetings Yvonne's boss will disagree with every idea she brings up, and Yvonne will not like the boss's ideas. So it is, six days a week.

Yvonne returns home mentally and physically exhausted.

Yvonne returns home mentally and physically exhausted. She eats a meager meal, opens a bedroom window to let in the evening air, and flops onto her bed.

She is drifting into sleep, when a mocking bird begins singing its heart out by the open window. The mocking bird sings a lovely array of songs.

Yvonne lies quietly for a while, listening and marveling at the mocking bird's skill. "You are lucky to be a bird and not a human," says Yvonne to the mocking bird. "For as a bird, you have an easy life with few worries."

"You have an easy life with few worries," sings the mocking bird.

Yvonne sits up, now fully awake. "What did you just say?" asks Yvonne.

"What did you just say?" sings the mocking bird.

"Do you know what I am saying?" tries Yvonne again.

"Do you know what I am saying?" sings the mocking bird.

"Hmph!" snorts Yvonne. "You're a mocking bird. You just repeat everything you hear."

"You're a mocking bird," sings the mocking bird. "You just repeat everything you hear. Human, do you think it is so easy to live life as a bird?"

Yvonne is astonished to hear the mocking bird speaking its own mind.

"It is you humans that have the easy life," continues the mocking bird. "You have a nice warm place to roost, with a built-in larder and water-hole. The advantages you have over birds are too numerous to name. Would you give them up and switch places with me?"

"Yes!" blurts Yvonne. "Yes, I would."

"So be it," says the mocking bird. "Give me a lock of your hair."

Yvonne gets a pair of scissors, cuts a lock of her hair, and presents it to the mocking bird.

The mocking bird places Yvonne's hair on its head. It then

pulls out one of its feathers and presents it to Yvonne. "Put my feather in your hair," directs the mocking bird.

Yvonne places the feather in her hair, and quicker than a lightning flash, she and the mocking bird switch bodies.

"This is wonderful!" squeals Yvonne.

"I think," says the mocking bird, "that by the time a year has passed you will feel differently."

"Not likely," says Yvonne.

"As you say," says the mocking bird. "Even so, return here in a year's time. Until then take good care of my body."

"Oh I will!" promises Yvonne. "And you take good care of mine."

"Rest assured," replies the mocking bird, with a smile, "you shall be well taken care of."

Yvonne spreads her wings and soars gleefully away. She stretches her wings across the countryside until it gets too dark for her to see her way. Finding a sheltered spot, Yvonne settles down to sleep.

Meanwhile, the mocking bird is raiding Yvonne's pantry. It gorges itself with all manner of goodies and then it lumbers to the bed where it snores through the night.

When the morning comes, Yvonne is ravenously hungry. She flies until she sees a house with a back-yard vegetable garden. Yvonne lands and tries one vegetable after another, but she finds them all distasteful and unsatisfying. Although it turns her stomach, she knows that a fat, juicy earthworm is what she needs.

Yvonne is not a good forager, and by the time she spies an earthworm, she is ready to eat just about anything. Her beak waters in anticipation. She pecks up the worm, gulps it down, and finds it to her liking. Yvonne is quickly adapting to bird-life.

Back in the city, the mocking bird is adjusting to its life as a human. It has managed to wash, dress, and catch a taxi to Yvonne's place of work. How, you ask? Well, the mocking bird has observed humans for years and is well versed in their ways and customs. He now sits in a meeting with Yvonne's boss.

"Well, Yvonne," says the boss, "those are my ideas. What do you think?"

"What do you think?" says the mocking bird.

"I like them a lot," says the boss.

"I like them a lot," says the mocking bird.

"I am glad to hear that," says the boss.

"I am glad to hear that," says the mocking bird.

"Now is a good time to tell you, Yvonne," says the boss, "that I am raising your pay."

"Thank you," says the mocking bird.

The year passes quickly for Yvonne who has traveled most of the globe in her feathered form. Now, she is again perched on the windowsill of her former apartment.

The mocking bird sees Yvonne, and raises the bedroom window. "Yvonne," says the mocking bird, "give me a feather. You were right; humans do have a more difficult life than birds. Give me a feather and let us regain our former bodies."

"I've been so many places," says Yvonne, "and I've seen such wondrous sights!"

"That's nice," says the mocking bird. "Give me a feather."

"And," continues Yvonne, "I've quite gotten used to a diet of worms, insects, and berries!"

"Yvooone...," says the mocking bird with impatience and suspicion.

"Well," says Yvonne. "Uh. The truth is, you see, I like being a bird and have no desire to return to my former self. You can keep my body. Bye-bye!"

Yvonne flaps off into the sunset, and the mocking bird watches in wide-eyed and open-mouthed dismay.

Years later, the mocking bird is still trapped in Yvonne's human form. It is lying on a bed, exhausted from a day at the office. Through the open window it hears a bird singing its melodious songs. "You birds have an easy life," says the mocking bird to the singing bird.

The bird stops singing. "You humans are all alike," says the songbird sourly. "You think being a bird is all fun and frolic. If you would change places with me, just give me a lock of your hair."

Even before the songbird can finish its sentence, the mocking bird is tripping over one piece of furniture after another as it makes a headlong dash for a pair of scissors.≡

Peas Please

*T*his is Susan. Susan just loves peas. She can't get enough and eats them with gusto. If it were up to her, she would have peas for breakfast, lunch, and dinner.

One day Susan's mother runs out of peas. She soon discovers the grocery store is also out of peas. In fact no one in the whole town has peas, not even the local farmers. It is a bad year for the pea crops.

Susan is overcome with grief. How can she live without peas? So bothered is she by this thought, that she cries herself to sleep.

The next morning she awakens to the aroma of oatmeal being cooked. Yuck! The unpleasant thought of eating oatmeal, makes her stomach churn. However, as soon as Susan puts her spoon into her bowl, **POOF**, the oatmeal changes to peas. Susan doesn't know how she did this, but she is very happy. She eats every last pea.

The same thing happens at lunch time. Her peanut butter and jelly sandwich turns into peas at her slightest touch. Dinner is no different. Instead of tuna surprise, Susan has peas.

What a wonderful day it has been for Susan. To have all of the peas she wants is glorious! She drifts happily to sleep.

The next day is a repeat of the last. No matter what meal is placed before Susan, as soon as she touches her food, **POOF**, it becomes peas. Susan is as happy as a lark; that is until six months later, when she still can only eat peas. Susan's once perky shoulders are now quite droopy as she eyes her plate of peas.

As surprising as it may sound, Susan has become tired of eating only peas for every meal. There seems to be nothing she or anyone else can do about it. Spaghetti with sauce, hot and buttered corn on the cob, apple pie with cinnamon ice cream, even steamed cauliflower, all turn into peas at Susan's touch. She used to hate steamed cauliflower, but now she longs to taste it. Her friends and family avoid her, for fear that she will turn their food into peas.

Susan is overcome with grief. How can she live on just peas? So bothered is she by this thought, that she cries herself to sleep.

The next morning Susan awakes to the smell of peas being cooked for her breakfast. It is just as well, since everything will turn to peas anyway. Susan seats herself at the kitchen table. As soon as her spoon touches her peas, **POOF**, they are turned into steamed cauliflower.

Susan is elated! She eats every bit of the steamed cauliflower, with all of the energy she can muster. She even licks the plate. Susan does not care if she ever sees another pea. As far as she is concerned, steamed cauliflower tastes ever so much better than peas.

We will come back and see her…in six months.≡

The Predictions

*R*upert is spending the day at the carnival, hoping it will lift his spirits. He recently lost his job and is feeling mighty low. The carnival is doing little to buoy him up. A roller coaster ride following his consumption of a tainted hotdog has him feeling lower than when he first arrived. It's time he headed home.

On his way out, Rupert sees a fortuneteller's tent, and on impulse decides to go in for a reading. Within the darkened tent is a woman who looks as old as time. She is seated at a round table on which is a ball of crystal.

"I have been expecting you," she says, in a voice that sounds like pieces of sandpaper being rubbed together. She gestures to a seat with the wave of a bangled arm. "Sit down and I will tell you of the things to come."

Rupert is troubled by the old fortuneteller's words. How is it that she had known he was coming? He only just a moment ago decided to have a reading. With trepidation he sits in the seat across from her, ready to bolt from the tent if the need arises.

71

The old woman places her hands around the crystal ball, until they are almost touching it. Then her hands swarm about the ball. She closes her eyes and begins a low chant. The ball starts to glow dully. The fortuneteller sways from side to side and the ball glows brighter and brighter. Just when the light from the ball becomes almost unbearable to look upon, and Rupert is about to run from the tent, her eyes snap open. She peers deeply into the ball, and speaks in a voice that resonates commandingly throughout the tent.

"I see in your future," she announces, "that you will win a brand new car. You will meet a beautiful woman and she will move in with you. Ahh! I see you being presented with a million dollars." Peering more deeply she says, "I see that you will live for a long time in a very expensive and very big house."

The light fades from the crystal ball, signaling the end of the reading. "That will be ten dollars," says the fortuneteller while extending her bejeweled hand.

"Ha!" scoffs Rupert as he reluctantly hands the old woman ten dollars, "It seems that I have wasted not only my time but my money as well. Old woman, those things only happen to men with luck. I am the most unlucky man you shall ever meet. Good day to you Grandmother." Rupert heads for the exit.

"The crystal ball does not lie!" calls the fortuneteller. "You shall see!"

By the time Rupert gets to his car, he has forgotten all about the old fortuneteller. He is just pulling out of the carnival's parking lot, when his car is hit from the rear by another vehicle. Rupert escapes without injury, but his car is totaled. It is fortunate that the other driver has auto insurance. The insurance company replaces Rupert's "junker" with a brand new car.

Rupert is test driving his new car when he sees, on the sidewalk, a young lady who has broken a heel on one of her high-heeled shoes. She is quite beautiful and loaded down with packages from some recent shopping trip. It is obvious that she is in great distress.

Rupert pulls to the curb and offers to give her a lift. She accepts, on the condition Rupert lets her treat him to lunch as recompense. Rupert agrees.

They have their lunch date, and several more after that. It isn't long before the young lady moves in with Rupert. Rupert is beside himself with happiness, until one day he comes home and finds his apartment empty.

Everything has been taken, even his aquarium and goldfish. The young lady is nowhere to be seen, she did not even bother to leave a note. Rupert wonders how it is that he can be so unlucky. Surely his luck will soon change for the better.

Rupert is walking through the park lamenting his plight, when a man runs up to him and thrusts a suitcase into his arms. The man then sprints away. Rupert is greatly puzzled by this, and overcome with curiosity he opens the suitcase. Inside the case is more money than Rupert has ever dreamed of seeing. "There must be a million dollars here!" he exclaims with excitement.

It is while he is exclaiming over the cash that the police arrive. They see Rupert hovering over the suitcase full of money, and they slap handcuffs onto his wrists. Rupert's protests are ignored as he is hauled downtown.

At the court trial, the jury finds Rupert guilty of unlawful possession of a million dollars and of trying to elude the police. The judge passes a sentence that will have Rupert spending the next thirty years in jail. He will live for a long time at a new one hundred million dollar state-of-the-art facility known as the "Big House".

Rupert now shuffles slowly through the chow line in his new state-of-the-art home. As he does so, he reflects on the old seer's predictions. As she foretold he was given a brand new car, he met a beautiful woman and she moved in with him, he was presented with a million dollars, and now he will live for a long time in a very expensive and very big house. "Those things only happen to men with luck", he says to the bemused food server who is at that moment plopping a large helping of odious slop onto a plate which he hands to Rupert.

Rupert is the most unlucky man you shall ever meet.≡

Seth the Sea Walker

Seth has a dilemma. In a week's time his grandmother, with whom he lives, will lose her farm. She has no money with which to pay the mortgage, and there is no one in a position to lend her the money. Seth will try to do what he can, to help his poor grandmother, but the future looks dim.

Seth decides to try to raise money by chopping and selling firewood. It is very hard work chopping logs to a size that can be burned within a fireplace, and before long he is tired and sore. He wipes sweat from his brow, takes a seat on the chopping block, and studies the small pile of firewood his efforts have produced. "I'd better find some other way to save the farm", he says to himself.

Next he helps the neighboring farmers bring in their crops. This is still hard work, though not as hard as chopping firewood. It takes an awfully long time to bring in the harvest, and the resulting pay is minuscule.

Time is running out. As he slumps on a pile of straw in the barn, Seth prays for a miracle. He knows there must be some way to get grandma the money.

Just then, he spies his grandfather's old diving suit and waterproof lantern. At the same moment he remembers the stories his grandfather told him about the old treasure-bearing ships. Many had sunk off the coast during frightful storms. For years grandfather had searched for the fabled treasure, but only ever came home with a few plates and pots sifted from the sea's bottom.

Seth gazes thoughtfully at the diving suit. His grandfather had been a very clever man and had fashioned the suit to hold enough air such that the wearer could remain submerged for long lengths of time. Seth picks up the suit's headpiece. It is his last chance to save his grandmother's farm. When night comes, Seth, carrying the suit and lantern, slips away. It will take him until sunrise to reach the coast.

Once at the coast, Seth dons the diving suit, takes up his lantern, and cautiously enters the water. The water is cold around his knees, even colder around his waist. He continues until he is deep under the sea. It is slow going, for with each step the sticky sea mud threatens to suck off his weighted boots.

He can see many strange and beautiful sights by the light of his lamp. Little fish drawn by the light investigate his legs and tickle them with their fins.

Seth searches for a long time without finding anything of value. He is tired and hungry. "A few more minutes", he thinks, "and then I will head back to shore."

He is just about to turn around when he finds it…a small treasure box half buried in the sea muck. Seth's heart leaps in his chest. He hoists up the box and retraces his steps to the shore.

He is almost there, when he feels something wrap around his ankle. It is a playful octopus. Seth does not feel much like playing and frantically struggles to free himself.

During his struggles the bottom of the treasure box gives way. The contents float to the muck below.

After what seems like an eternity, Seth frees himself and emerges from the sea. Panting and weeping in frustration, he throws himself onto the sand. He has failed. He had the salvation of his grandmother's farm within his grasp and has lost it. And so the farm too is lost.

He removes the diving gear and makes his way home. It is nighttime and the moon is high, full, and bright by the time Seth arrives home. How can he face his grandmother after losing such a treasure?

Seth lies on the straw in the barn. The moonlight shines through a window and illuminates the muddy bottoms of the diving boots. Sparkly lights of green, red, and gold wink and twinkle. Seth jumps to his feet and pounces on the boots.

In the mud are emeralds, rubies, and gold. They had been imbedded in the sticky mud on his boots, during his struggles with the octopus. It is a joyous moment for Seth, but it is too late to save the farm.

In Seth's absence, his grandmother was forced to sign away the farm. She mistakenly thought that she had more time than she actually did.

Do not grieve for them however, for now they are wealthy and live happily on a beautiful farm in the neighboring county. Thanks to Seth the Sea Walker.≡

Travelers

𝕿wo men, strangers to each other, find themselves traveling the same road. They walk side by side for a time before exchanging pleasantries. One goes by the name of Horsa and the other Stigand. As many travelers do when they find they are going in the same direction, Horsa and Stigand form an unspoken friendship. They walk a little further before deciding to rest their tired feet. While they are seated at the side of the road they espy an elderly man.

The elderly man, his frame bent from years of toil, is pushing a handcart. As he approaches the seated pair, the aroma of his cargo precedes him, fresh, ripe nectarines. His cart is laden with them.

The pair's mouths ache for want of the sweet smelling nectarines from the elder's cart. "Hey, old man," says Horsa when the elder is within earshot, "we have not had anything to eat today. Give us some of your nectarines."

The man rolls his cart until he is even with pair before saying, "I cannot. All of these nectarines are spoken for. The person to whom I deliver them is a most particular person and will know if any nectarines are missing from the cart. I have only two extras as replacements for fruits that may get lost or damaged along the way. However, back down the road a piece is a nectarine orchard, which I own. If you arrive there later and help me with some chores, I will be happy to give you nectarines as payment." Having explained the situation and offered fruits for labor, the elder leans his weight into the cart to continue on his way. He is only a few paces from the pair when, unbeknownst to him, two plump nectarines tumble from the cart.

Horsa sees them at once, but waits until the old man is well away before rushing over to snatch up the fruits. Striding back he says, "Look here! We have nectarines without the backbreaking labor."

When Stigand sees the two fruits, he leaps to his feet and, grabbing the nectarines, sprints after the old man. He catches the oldster and extends the fruits saying, "Sir, these fruits have fallen from your cart."

"Thank ye," says the man. "My offer to come to my orchard still stands." He nods a goodbye and off he goes.

Horsa, puffing slightly, comes to stand beside Stigand. "Now why did you have to go and do that?" Horsa asks.

"Those nectarines belong to another," replies Stigand. "Did you not hear him say the person to whom he is taking the nectarines is of a particular sort? The old man may be beaten or branded a cheat and run out of the village. For the want of two nectarines the old man could be ruined. We shall have nectarines soon enough."

Horsa groans and squeezes his empty belly.

Later in the day when they arrive at the orchard, they are put to work gathering dead branches, picking up rotting fruit, and various other tasks. Stigand throws himself into his labors, but Horsa moves reluctantly through the orchard doing only the easiest tasks. When the sun begins to set, work ceases and the two are given ten nectarines each. The fruits are flawless, at their peak ripeness, and smell wonderful.

"There is always something to be done in an orchard," says the elder, as the two ready themselves to leave. "If you have a mind to come back tomorrow, there will be more work and more nectarines waiting for you."

That evening, Horsa and Stigand enjoy their nectarines so much that even before the rooster crows they are again at the elder's orchard ready to lend a hand. This goes on for many days. Stigand always attacks his tasks energetically and, by listening intently to what the elder has to say, absorbs much about orchard culture.

Each day Horsa moves lethargically through the orchard seeming to take no interest in its culture, but biding his time until the elder portions out nectarines.

The lopsided work ethic of the pair has not escaped the eyes of the elder, but he says nothing as he doles out fruits.

One day, after the day's work has come to a close, the elder says, "Tomorrow I shall spend the day within the village selling nectarines from my cart to passersby. It is a task I must perform if I am to pay the king's taxes." In truth the oldster will lose this beloved orchard that has been in his family for generations, if he fails to satisfy when the taxman visits. "You may work if you wish," continues the elder, "and pluck fruits as recompense."

"Why not let us take your fruits into the village?" offers Stigand. "There are two of us so we can take two cart loads."

This idea is amenable to the elder, and so the morrow finds Horsa and Stigand peddling nectarines in the village.

The village is crowded this market day and the only spaces left for Horsa and Stigand have their carts some distance away from each other. Horsa sets up closest to the market's entrance and the aroma of delectable nectarines draws one customer after another. However, Horsa's attitude is not conducive to making sales. "Ah! Nectarine Monger," says a prospective buyer. "How fine your nectarines smell. Are they for sale?"

"And why else do you think I hauled them to market?" Horsa retorts.

The patron gives Horsa a look that is a mixture of surprise, confusion, and disapproval. He turns on his heels and strides away, having no desire to purchase nectarines from a surly lout.

At the end of the market day, Stigand parks his empty cart in front of the elder's abode. He hands him a sack of coins before receiving ten large nectarines for his day's work.

Horsa wheels his cart to the rear of the elder's abode and parks it there. The only fruits missing from his cart are the ones he himself ate throughout the day. He has not a copper to present to the elder, but the elder says not a word as he gives Horsa his ten promised nectarines.

The next time Horsa and Stigand venture into the village for a selling session Stigand takes with him a saucepot and a stout stick.

Once situated in the market, Stigand bangs the saucepot with the stick to get the attention of passersby. His efforts prove fruitful, as soon a throng is vying for his produce. Even though he has increased his asking price, he sells out quickly.

While Stigand is drumming up business, Horsa lounges and eats unsold produce.

The old man is pleased when Stigand presents him with a weighty sack of coins. The oldster is glad to have the help, so does not chide Horsa concerning the fruit he consumes or the coins he does not bring. Each receives their fruity fee.

For the third market outing Stigand plucks nectarines in the cool of the morning and insulates them well with straw. Within the straw the nectarines retain their chill even when the midday's heat arrives, thus they are a tasty and cooling treat. Stigand raises his price again and acquires a large profit on his harvest.

Even Horsa decides to make an effort and sells most of his offerings. He grins as he counts the earnings, and looks left and right before secreting away several coins for himself.

When given Stigand's portion of the day's takings, the elder is lost for words. Tears of gratitude stream down his wrinkled cheeks and drip to the ground.

The scene of the teary-eyed elder has a profound effect on Horsa. So much so that Horsa adds his stash of coins to the sack before passing it over. Not only that. In the weeks that follow, Horsa eagerly toils tirelessly at the most difficult chores.

The nectarines continue to sell well at market, enabling the elder to pay the taxman in full and have quite a bit of money besides.

There comes an occasion when the elder calls the two to him and says, "I truly love this orchard, but I am unable to administer the care and maintenance as I did in the past. I have no heir who will lay claim to it, so I have signed the deed over to you." So saying he hands the deed to Stigand. "I know I leave it in good hands."

"I-I thank you, sir!" says Stigand, genuinely surprised. "Your orchard will receive the attentive care it deserves."

The elder musters a tired smile and, to Horsa's and Stigand's amazement, fades out of existence. Some days later as they sweat within the orchard, they come across the resting place of the elder's bones. It seems the elder had returned in spectral form to do what he could not in life, find one suitable to inherit the orchard. His mission complete, he can rest easily.

"Horsa," says Stigand, as he gazes at the mound of earth, "I have decided that come the morrow I shall resume my travels. On the deed to this orchard I shall sign your name."

These are words Horsa had not expected to hear. He eyes the soil for a long time before saying, "No. Both our names must be signed to the deed. It is only right that half belong to you."

Stigand clamps Horsa on the shoulder by way of agreement.

Stigand's travels take him far and wide. Meanwhile, Horsa amasses wealth as a fruit monger. Every day he can be found caring for the orchard as one might a cherished gift. And so it is, a gift which will remain fruitful long after his bones are laid to rest.≡

Troll's Treat

O ddvar of Scandinavia is off to seek his fortune in a distant land. So eager is he to reach his destination, he unwisely decides to take a dangerous shortcut. The shortcut spells danger for all travelers who traipse its treacherous mountainous pass, for a hungry troll lies in wait for hapless humans. Oddvar has full knowledge of this, but is willing to take the risk to shave time from his trek.

He makes great progress, right up to the point where massive, hairy hands seize him from behind. Oddvar tries to run, but it is of no use. A stocky, short-limbed troll, whose thick hands are as large as serving platters, binds him with a grip so strong, no mortal man could hope to break it.

"Ya-ha-ha," laughs the troll wickedly, exposing two rows of yellow-green teeth. "Ya-ha-ha-ha-ha-haaa!" The troll spends a great deal of time laughing, for at that moment he is extremely happy. It is not every day he can lay his hairy hands upon a human, so he feels it is cause for celebration.

"Ah!" says Oddvar. "Friend Troll. I had begun to think I would never find you."

"What?" inquires the troll, quite bemused.

"I have searched high and low for you," says Oddvar. "How strange that it is you who finds me. My name is Oddvar. Now that we have met..."

"Now that we have met," growls the troll, "it is too bad for you." He gives Oddvar a piercing gaze and drool glistens down his chin. While keeping a tight hold, the troll begins to gather and pile sticks. When he deems the pile to be sufficient, he tops it with a large cookpot.

Oddvar has no trouble guessing his fate. He combs the corners of his mind for a way out of his dilemma, but finds nothing. He knows all too well that trolls, above everything, enjoy eating. It is not likely the troll will pass up the chance of a tasty meal. Finally, a thought comes to him and he begins to laugh. He laughs with wild energy.

The troll, momentarily surprised by Oddvar's raucous laughter, releases his hold. Wrapped in laughter Oddvar falls to the earth. The troll stares at him, not knowing what to make of the situation. "Human!" says the troll. "Do you not know what fate I have in store for you?"

"Oh yes," replies Oddvar, through his mirth and tears.

"And you find it amusing?" asks the troll.

In answer, Oddvar guffaws even louder, holds his belly, and drums his feet upon the ground.

The troll becomes angry. He snatches Oddvar up and gives him a shake. "Tell me, human, why do you find such joy in the fact that you will soon be in my cookpot?"

"I have heard," says Oddvar, while wiping moisture from his eyes, "that trolls have appetites as deep as a bottomless pit."

"Yes," confesses the troll, "it is so."

"Well," says Oddvar, "put me in your pot and you will have one meager meal. However, release me and you will have as many delicious meals as your belly will hold."

The troll says not a word. In his silence he shifts his gaze repeatedly from the cookpot to Oddvar. At length he says, "Alright, human. I shall release you, but do not forget my cookpot stands ready for use."

"And it is a good thing too," says Oddvar, "for I have need of it. First I must forage for ingredients."

"Acquire your ingredients," snarls the troll, "but do not seek to escape. Do not try to trick me and do not go too far away. I have keen eyesight and I shall be watching your every move. Try to flee and I will gobble you up in an instant!"

"No need to bluster," says Oddvar. "I shall not try to escape."

In truth trolls have very keen senses, ten times that of the average human. The huge eyes, nose, ears, and lips that protrude from the troll's shaggy head miss nothing. No, Oddvar will not get far if he tries to betray the troll.

While foraging, Oddvar finds a small pool of water which contains fallen leaves, decomposing bark, mud, and a multitude of mosquito larvae. He fills a vessel, which he has borrowed from the troll, with the liquid. Taking it to the troll, he says, "Here. A little something to refresh you."

The troll takes the proffering and swigs it. "Mmmm!" exclaims the troll. "What a refreshing drink. It is very flavorful and it tickles my throat as it goes down." That would be the wriggling mosquito larvae.

Further foraging yields several expired forest creatures in advanced stages of ripeness. Oddvar puts them, along with various roots, nuts, and a quantity of water into the pot. The pile of sticks is set aflame and after a while the mixture releases a powerful odor.

The troll keeps a close eye on the burbling stew. The pool of drool at his feet evidences his anticipation of the coming feast. However, he is made to wait until the stew is at the peak of perfection, by which time the troll is on his knees begging for permission to eat.

"Come and get it," says Oddvar.

The troll, unmindful of the pot's intense heat, grabs the pot with both hands and tips it toward his gaping mouth. "Oohhh..." coos the troll with delight before taking another pull at the pot. "Ohh, this is good." He finishes the stew and licks the pot clean. "Ahh!" He exhales and reclines upon the ground. A moment later a curious thing happens. The troll increases in size. It is a slight increase, but an increase nonetheless. Oddvar takes note of it.

"I am glad I spared you," says the troll. "I have never before tasted such delicious fare."

"That is nothing," says Oddvar. "Just wait until you taste all that I have in store for you."

The troll opens his mouth in a grin and begins to drool.

"But first," says Oddvar, "you must perform a task for me."

The troll narrows his eyes in suspicion.

"Hauling all of the ingredients for which I forage is heavy and time-consuming work. I could forage faster if I had a wheeled cart."

In short order the troll fashions a cart from a slab of wood and some logs.

"Oh," says Oddvar, when the troll is done, "what a fine cart. You are a very skilled craftsman."

The troll is pleased by the compliment.

"Now," says Oddvar, "you may go into your cave and rest while I go about preparing your next meal."

"Alright," says the troll, "but remember…"

"Yes I know," interrupts Oddvar, "you will be watching me." Oddvar prepares one meal after another, sleeping only as long as it takes for the pot to boil. He has convinced the troll that he need not trouble himself to come out of his cave to take his meals, for they will be delivered to him upon the wheeled cart. So it is that the troll passes weeks and weeks within the cave without ever stepping into the open air.

Finally, a day comes when Oddvar decides he will not cook another meal for the troll. When the troll bellows for something to eat, Oddvar says, "Quiet your bluster! You will get nothing more from me. If you would have something to eat, fetch it yourself."

"WHAT?" roars the troll, unsure his keen ears heard right. "I spared your life on your promise to feed me. Would you now betray your oath to fill my belly?"

"I know not the true capacity of your belly," says Oddvar, "but I think it is at this moment holding quite enough."

Indeed it does, for when the troll tries to move he finds he cannot. He has grown so large that his bulk fills the cave.

He fumes and threatens, but there is no way he can escape his dwelling.

"No," says Oddvar. "I have held my end of the bargain. It is your greed, which has betrayed you, and it is on that you may chew when you are with hunger." With that Oddvar turns and walks away.

The troll rages mightily as he watches Oddvar go. His efforts to escape his confinement are heroic, setting the ground quaking for great distances. However, they yield him nothing. He whimpers weakly.

It is doubtful the troll will expire within the cave. For trolls can live to be hundreds of years old. Be that as it may, it will be a long, long, very long time before he shrinks enough to exit the cave. When that time comes he is sure to be hungry. And he mournfully reflects that in his anger he did not think to ask Oddvar for his scrumptious recipes.≡

The Two Brothers

𝒶n aging Slavic farmer and his wife have two sons, Sasha and Yuri. Yuri is the eldest and he wishes to marry his sweetheart who lives not too far away. "Father," says Yuri to his father, "I wish to take a wife and setup my own household. I have come to ask for your blessing and a portion of the family holdings."

The father looks at his eldest through the tired but knowing eyes of one whose ancestors have farmed the land for generations. He too feels it is time for his son to establish his own family. "You shall have my blessing and a portion of the family holdings," says the father, "on one condition. Your brother also has a desire to marry and your mother and I feel that the time is right. Since there are no daughters yet unmarried in these parts, he must go on a quest to find his maiden. Take him and, as you are more knowing than he in the ways of courtship, help him choose wisely."

"But, Father," protests Yuri, "I--"

"That is my condition," interrupts the father. "Help your brother."

"Yes, Father," says Yuri.

Sasha is delighted when he hears the news and, after packing a satchel of provisions, is soon traveling a road with his brother by his side.

The day wears on and as the sun slips below the horizon it begins to rain. It rains all night, a steady downpour, which soaks them thoroughly and dampens their spirits. By the middle of the afternoon of the next day the rain has stopped and they are slogging along the muddy road when they happen upon a gaily-painted covered wagon. The wagon is mired in mud and, to complicate matters further, it has a broken wheel.

The owner of the wagon is a traveling performer. His elderly form is slumped against the broken wheel, having exhausted himself and his horse by trying to move the heavy conveyance.

The brothers help the old man totter to a shady spot at the side of the road. Once situated the old performer says, "My thanks. The wagon's wheel is broken, and I..."

"No need to fret," interjects Sasha, "we will undertake the repair of your wagon."

The old man musters a weary smile in appreciation. "How fortunate I am that you two strapping lads happened upon me," he says. "Why, if I may ask, do you travel this lonely road?"

"We are on a quest to find for me a bride," says Sasha.

"Ah!" says the old man, perking up. "If it is a bride you are looking for, then you must meet my daughter."

"Is your daughter a beauty?" asks Yuri.

"You may search high and you may search low," replies the man theatrically, "but you will not find a more beauteous maiden than my daughter. I believe she is sleeping in the shade on the other side of the wagon. She should awaken soon and I shall introduce you to her."

"That will be fine," says Sasha. He notices how weak and hungry the elder man seems to be and so retrieves from his satchel flatbread and a length of sausage. "In the meantime, let us have something to eat."

While Sasha is busy dividing the bread and sausage, Yuri cannot resist the urge to sneak a glance at the sleeping maiden. What he sees freezes his marrow.

Snoring open-mouthed in the shade of the wagon is a female clothed in filthy rags. Her hair is matted and full of brambles, her nose is long and curves so that it almost meets with her chin, there are boils on her cheeks and forehead, and her slack jaw reveals blackened and crooked teeth.

"It is Baba Yaga, the witch!" exclaims Yuri in a hoarse whisper. Baba Yaga is known far and wide for her numerous wicked deeds against humanity.

Rushing to the other side of the wagon he grasps his brother's wrist in an iron grip and hauls him along saying, "It is time to go, brother!"

"Brother, what are you doing?" protests Sasha. "We have not yet eaten and the wagon still needs fixing! Brother! Brother, wait! The maiden, do you not wish to meet the beauteous maiden?"

At the mention of the maiden, Yuri breaks into a run. It is all Sasha can do to keep his footing as Yuri tows him along.

The brothers' hasty departure has the old man scratching his head in befuddlement. However, he and his daughter will not go hungry, as the younger has left behind flatbread, a sausage, and a gourd of drink.

It is the onset of exhaustion that forces Yuri to cease his flight. Both brothers collapse and pant heavily. "Have, have you gone mad, brother?" demands the gasping Sasha. "Why did we leave without helping the old man and his daughter? Brother?" He receives no reply, for his exhausted sibling has fallen fast asleep.

Long after the sun has set, Sasha remains awake thinking about the old man's plight. Finally he makes up his mind to retrace his steps to the wagon. In the far distance he sees a small campfire and so heads toward it. The fire is out and only glowing embers remain by the time he reaches the wagon. All is quiet. He presumes the old man and his daughter have turned in for the night. Working swiftly, and as silently as his straining sinews will allow, he replaces the broken wheel with the wagon's spare. When that is done, he spreads a cloth and leaves the last of his bread and sausage upon it before taking his leave. His whole attention is now given to navigating his way back to his sleeping brother, so he does not notice the old performer peering at him from the covered wagon and smiling approvingly.

By daybreak the brothers' bellies are grumbling with hunger. "Pass me the bread and sausages, brother," says Yuri. "We will break our fast before continuing our quest."

"There is no bread or sausage," says Sasha. "They have been left at the performer's wagon. All that remains in our rations satchel is a small jar of honey. Brother, why did we leave in such a hurry? I wish we could have stayed long enough to see the old man's daughter. He said she is quite beautiful."

Yuri shudders at the remembrance of the sleeping figure. "Brother," says Yuri, "all fathers proclaim their daughters great beauties." Yuri chooses not to impart the news that Sasha was almost suitor to Baba Yaga. "Enough about the performer's daughter. Since we are without rations I will go into yon woods," he says, pointing to a copse of trees, "and forage for food while you fill my gourd and gather fuel for a cook fire." The elder doffs his gourd and strides to the woods.

Despite his brother's words, Sasha still wishes to meet the old performer's daughter. Even if she is not a beautiful person without, as professed, she may be a beautiful person within, and in his mind that is the best beauty of all. He watches until Yuri is within the woodline before trotting to the site of the performer's wagon. The wagon has moved on. All that remains is a small straw sack. He stoops, opens the sack, and extracts a glass orb the size of a large apple. He holds the orb aloft and, peering into it, sees a swirling gray mist. "Hmph," he grunts in wonderment before inserting the orb into the sack and placing the sack's strap over one shoulder. He plans to give it back to the old performer if ever he should see him again.

Returning to his campsite he builds a fire, tops off his brother's gourd with water from a nearby stream, and waits for his brother to bring food. While he is waiting, his gurgling stomach beseeches him to retrieve the last of their rations, the little jar of honey. When he removes the wax lid the honey releases a delicious aroma, which causes his mouth to water. He is about to dip a forefinger into the jar when the sack containing the orb begins to writhe. He hastily removes the sack and tosses it aside.

With a grunt and a snuffle, a gigantic bear wriggles from the sack. Approaching Sasha, who is immobile with fright, the great bear laps honey from the jar. When the jar is empty the shaggy beast shambles to the stream, plunges in and, with powerful swipes of his paw, sends fish flying onto shore.

In a short time there is a mound of fish flopping at Sasha's feet. He can only gawk as the dripping bear wriggles back into the sack which, after a moment, lies still.

When Yuri returns with a handful of swamp tubers, he finds skewered fish sizzling over open flames. "Sasha, how did you catch all of these fish?" inquires Yuri, while gesturing to the feast.

Sasha, pointing to the straw sack and the orb in it, gives Yuri an account of the events which took place.

As he listens to the report, Yuri eyes the straw sack with suspicion. "What an interesting tale," says Yuri, wishing to hear no more about the strange orb. It is just as well that he had not witnessed the brawny bear's behavior with his own eyes. He knows the orb, if it came from the wagon where slept Baba Yaga, might well contain unfathomable magic. However, having no desire to tell his brother about the old witch, he chuckles and says, "Fish, be they from bear or man, are all the same to me so long as they sate my hunger."

The fish, tubers, and stream water make a surprisingly good breakfast. Once their bellies are full, they continue the quest. They travel for some distance before encountering a deep gorge.

The gorge was once negotiable via a rope bridge. However, the ropes on the side where the brothers now stand have come away from their mooring and dangle uselessly on the far side of the gap. "Wait here," says Yuri, "while I search for an alternate way across."

Yuri is gone for a short time when Sasha's belly grumbles. Instinctively he reaches for the satchel that once held their rations. He opens it, turns it upside down, and shakes it vigorously. For his efforts he is rewarded with a small mound of breadcrumbs.

He is contemplating the crumbs when an ant scuttles from the straw sack, picks up a crumb with its mandibles, and reenters the sack. Almost immediately, several more ants appear and do likewise until no crumbs remain. Of a sudden the sack begins to writhe. He hastily removes the sack and tosses it aside while half expecting the emergence of the honey-loving bear. It is not the snuffling bear that comes from the sack, this time it is ants.

Ants in mind-boggling numbers march from the sack and towards the gorge. The one-inch ants, linking their bodies one to another, extend to the bottom of the gorge; they crawl up the far side, and then tighten up to form a living bridge.

It is a long while before Sasha musters the nerve to set foot on the hymenopterous bridge. The bridge sags slightly under his weight, but holds. Moving carefully he crosses to the other side. He then retrieves the dangling ropes, and after crossing the bridge again, moors them securely. When this is completed, the multitudes of ants march back into the straw sack with the last ant entering as the eldest returns.

Yuri looks first at the repaired bridge, and then at his brother, and finally at the straw sack.

"Brother," exclaims Sasha, "shortly after you left--"

Yuri interrupts his brother by holding up the palm of his right hand. "No need to explain, brother," says Yuri, giving the straw sack a sidelong glance. "It is well enough that I only know we now have a crossing where not long ago there was none. Come. Let us be on our way, night is fast approaching and fog is on the rise."

During the night, the fog becomes so thick they cannot see more than a foot in front of them. "Maybe we should stop for the night, brother," says Sasha. "lest we lose each other."

"Don't worry," says Yuri, wanting to hasten the quest and be done with it, "we will be fine. Here, grasp the back of my tunic."

Sasha sniffs the damp air. "Do you smell that, brother?" asks Sasha.

"Smell what?" returns Yuri.

"That sweet fragrance," says Sasha. "It smells like...Ah! Here!" Stooping he plucks a handful of night-blooming flowers. "I shall give them to the old performer's daughter when next I see her."

"Brother," warns Yuri, "I do not think you--" His words are arrested, for at that instant a glowing firefly crawls from the straw sack, takes flight, and lands upon the plucked flowers. It sips nectar and gathers pollen before reentering the sack. A moment later, fireflies stream from the sack in droves. They fly ahead of the traveling pair and light the way using their bioluminescent bottoms.

"Mmm..." moans Yuri, as he squints at the fireflies. "Maybe you are right. We should wait until daybreak before continuing."

"There is no need to do that now, brother" returns Sasha excitedly. "For the fireflies light our path. This is a fortuitous occurrence." Yuri is not so sure of that.

The fireflies provide guidance until they encounter the glow of a lighted lantern, upon which they stream back into the straw sack.

The brothers approach the light. As they move closer Sasha's spirit soars and Yuri's spirit sinks, for the lantern hangs from the gaily-painted wagon belonging to the old performer.

"Hello again, lads," comes the old man's voice through the fog. "It seems our paths keep crossing."

"Indeed," says Yuri, dryly.

"We apologize for our hasty departure earlier," says Sasha.

"No apology needed," says the old man. "You must be really anxious to find a bride to travel on a night such as this."

Yuri coughs.

"Oh, where are my manners?" says the old performer. "Let me offer you something to drink." He calls to his daughter to bring three tankards of drink.

The daughter brings drink, which Yuri declines. While offering a tankard to Sasha her warm hand touches his. At that instant he senses all of the beauty and kindheartedness that is within her. He tries valiantly to see her features through the fog, but his efforts are futile. No matter, his heart is aflutter and, if she feels as he, then his quest has ended. He stuns his brother and pleases the old performer by asking for his daughter's hand in marriage.

The old man says he has an engagement in the next town, but promises to stop by the farm when his task is completed. Sasha gives him directions as Yuri listens open-mouthed and helpless.

On the trek back to their farm, Yuri tries to convince his brother that the performer's daughter is not the right choice. "Brother," says he, "you have been bewitched!"

"Mayhap you are right, brother," says Sasha. "I myself cannot truly explain what happened when our hands met, but I know I will have her to wife and no other."

It takes them several days to reach their farm upon which they impart the news that their quest has been successful. "Well done," says the father. Turning to the younger he says, "And what does your bride to be look like?"

"What matter looks," offers Sasha, "when the beauty in one's heart is foremost important?"

"True enough," returns the father.

"Uh, Father," says Yuri, "may I speak with you privately?" He will not get the chance, for a gaily-painted wagon pulls up and stops in front of their farmhouse.

The old performer drops down and greets the four. He calls for his daughter. "Come, Katinka, and meet he who wishes to marry you." His daughter steps from the wagon and the four farmers gasp and recoil.

"It is Baba Yaga!" wails the mother, covering her mouth and forehead in fright.

"This is how you help your brother?" roars the father.

"My daughter," says the old performer, "plays the part of the witch Baba Yaga during the skits we perform in various towns. She is a dedicated actress who stays in character even when sleeping." He turns to his daughter. "Daughter, you have played your last role as Baba Yaga. It is time to remove your makeup and take up your new role as wife and companion."

"Father," says Katinka, "why do you tease? Why do you say I wear makeup and that this is not my true form? Is it not Baba Yaga who stands before you? Who is so bold that he will wed Baba Yaga?"

"My daughter has a great sense of humor," says the old man, with a patient smile.

The old performer's smile broadens as Sasha steps forward to clasp the daughter's hands in his. The feel of her hands causes his heart to soar just as it did before on that foggy night. "Here is my bride," he announces, "I will have no other."

Katinka blushes deeply and shyly turns her head to one side. In the next moment she peels away her makeup and reveals a face that is youthful, radiant, and strikingly lovely.

The farmer, his wife, and Yuri exhale with great relief that they will not be in-laws to Baba Yaga.

As the farmer and old performer discuss the details concerning the coming marriage, Yuri pulls his brother to one side and says, "Brother, about that straw sack you carry..."

"Ah, yes," says Sasha. "I almost forgot." "Sir," he says to his soon to be father-in-law, "this straw sack, I believe, fell from your wagon. I wish to return it to you."

"Don't return it to me," says the performer. "It was given to my daughter many years ago by her great grandmother and it is now part of her dowry. The sack's contents may prove useful to you someday."

"In truth," says Sasha, "it already has."

"Indeed?" says the old performer with a knowing smile.

Yuri moves to stand beside the old performer. "Um, your daughter's great grandmother," inquires Yuri, "what is her name?"

"Need you ask?" replies the performer, whose words cause Yuri to turn pale.

There is a big celebration and wedding feast on the day of the brothers' dual matrimony, after which each lives happily on their portion of land and prosper until the end of their days.≡

The Wolf and the Sheep

High in the moonlit Alps, a shepherd, wrapped in a woolen cloak against the night's chill, watches over his flock. He shivers slightly and tugs his garment more tightly about him. As he does so he eyes the hound sleeping soundly at his feet and yawns mightily, fogging the air with his exhalation. Leaning heavily on his shepherd's crook, he reflects upon the peaceful and uneventful life he leads. It is a life into which he was born, but he has a mind to give up his peaceful existence for something more exciting while he is yet young enough to enjoy it. But then who would tend the flock?

The shepherd fills his lungs with crisp air before expelling it into an alp horn. The subsequent blast from the horn animates the cud-chewing sheep and they migrate swiftly to cluster about him.

Of a sudden the sheep bleat with alarm and flee pell-mell. The hound rouses itself and the hairs on its neck and back bristle. There is danger. Wolves!

Wolves have arrived and they have brought with them hearty appetites. Having been checked by man; wolves have not been seen in these parts for at least a hundred years. Yet, twelve slavering, yellow-eyed wolves harry the flock.

The shepherd, although greatly astonished, instinctively rushes to interpose himself between his sheep and members of the wolf pack. An instant passes before he realizes the folly of his action, but it is already too late, for the wolves are now giving him their full attention. The shepherd makes to pucker his quivering lips and whistle for his hound, but bothers not when he espies his sheepdog's silhouette high-tailing it over a distant hill.

The shepherd's face turns stony. With hands steadied by resolve, he settles his crook-necked staff into a defensive position against the snarling beasts. He will not surrender his sheep without making a good account of himself. The wolves, he vows, will not find him easy prey.

The canines' needle-sharp teeth gleam white by the moon's light. They gather themselves to leap, but falter as an awful, bowel-churning howl pierces the night. Confusion scatters their wits and before they can collect them, they find themselves tumbling paws over snouts, bowled over by a juggernaut. For a moment the wolves are a blur of fur and teeth as they jockey for dominance. The moment quickly passes. The stunned, sprawled wolves, when their vision clears, behold a massive black-gray wolf; its face ugly with contortions, its hackles raised, its legs splayed.

The black-gray is more than twice the size of a common wolf; it has red eyes that flare like twin fires, teeth longer than a man's digits, and thick fur that does little to conceal the abundant corded muscles that bunch beneath. His growl is a menacing baritone.

The marauding wolves have never before beheld such as the great black-gray and they are affrighted. Their alpha male makes to approach the black-gray, but yowls instead. The yowl is in reaction to a lightning-fast lunge from the giant wolf, which pins the alpha male to the earth. The alpha male whimpers under the bulk of the black-gray.

For long moments the smoldering red orbs of the snarling black-gray bore into those of the alpha male and there crosses an undeniable understanding between them. He then releases the prostrate wolf and emits a short, commanding bark. He need not have bothered to bark, for the pack has already scampered halfway across the dale, for they know here the black-gray is master.

The immense wolf once himself had a master, a minor wizard who, now centuries gone, lies skeletal in his stone crypt. One evening, while he yet breathed and when great boredom was upon him, the wizard had mumbled an incantation, which gave his wolf longevity and the ability to cloak itself in the guise of a sheep. It had not occurred to the wizard that animals would not be fooled by the illusion. Today the wolf had arrived wearing his former master's illusionary gift. So it is no surprise that when he turns to face the shepherd, the shepherd's wide eyes gaze upon an enormous red-eyed, fleecy ram.

The shepherd still holds his staff at the ready, but his whole being is soaked in sweat and he exudes the pungent odor of fear, which is so easily detected by wild beasts.

The wolf, in an effort to put the shepherd at ease, grins. This reveals yet another shortcoming with the illusionary spell, for at the sight of the oversized canines and incisors, below red orbs that glow as do red-hot coals, the shepherd trembles mightily and nearly faints.

Black-gray, seeing the unintended effect of his grin clears his throat and utters in his rich baritone, "Be at ease, Shepherd, I mean you no harm," All animals share a common language, but few of mankind realize animals can also understand and some even speak the human language. Animals prefer not to have it known they can speak to humans, but it will be revealed under extenuating circumstances such as now.

The shepherd turns pale upon hearing intelligible words issuing from the sharp-toothed maw. Fright heightens his sight and it breaches the wolf's ram façade. It is all too much for the quaking shepherd. His eyes glaze over, he swoons and he collapses to the ground to lie as a sack of grain.

One turn of the hourglass later, he regains consciousness. The big wolf, having dropped his disguise, is seated a respectable distance away. "Ah, Shepherd," says the wolf, "you have awakened. I say again, I mean you no harm. In fact, I am here to offer you my assistance."

"Assistance?" asks the shepherd, careful not to make any sudden movements while slowly propping himself onto an elbow.

"Yes," replies the wolf. "As you have witnessed, this area is fraught with marauding wolves. Wolves who, unlike me, mean you harm. Against such menaces one man cannot hope to prevail. So I shall watch over your flock. You have already seen I am up to the task."

The shepherd cannot help studying the double row of sharp teeth as he listens to the wolf's proposition. He considers his options, none of which he finds savory. He sighs. "Alright, wolf" he says. "I can see no other way to provide protection for my flock. I will give you charge if you prove you can sound yon alp horn."

"Alp horn?" says the wolf.

"Yes," replies the shepherd. "It is an instrument you can use, should the need arise, to summon me from the village." He approaches the elongated wooden horn, puts its mouthpiece to his lips and plays a long, mournful note.

The wolf's initial attempts at horn blowing are unsuccessful, but he perseveres. On his fifteenth attempt he replicates the tone produced by the shepherd, and does it thrice more to prove he has mastered the horn. "There, Shepherd," says the black-gray, "you may now retire to your den."

"I shall return in three days to see how you fare," says the shepherd. With that he takes his leave, not once looking back.

The wolf watches until the shepherd is lost from sight. "Foolish shepherd," sneers the wolf, as he saunters towards a group of frolicking lambs.

"What is in thy mind, wolf?" This voice comes from behind the wolf.

The wolf is startled and bridles as he stops in his tracks. He growls low in his throat as he turns, and then yelps in surprise. Standing before him are one hundred large, horned sheep. The wolf swallows hard...twice. Although each of the yellow-eyed sheep comprising the assemblage is only half the size of he, the wolf cannot stifle a nervous yawn.

"Ahh..." says the wolf, while trying to think quickly. "Why, uh...to introduce myself to yon lambs and mayhap play a few games with them", as soon as the words leave his muzzle, he is at once infused with shame and humiliation. Even so, he is no match for the horned horde and so will bide his time.

"Alright," says one of the glaring sheep evenly. "That and naught more, wolf."

The lambs in their innocence are delighted to have a wolf as a playmate. They bite his ears, tug his tail, bop his nose and leap upon his back as they play tag, hop the rock, and "ride the wolf". The playing continues until the lambs are dozy, just as the sun peeks above the horizon.

The Wolf and the Sheep

The wolf, his head and tongue hanging low, begins to make his way on shaky legs to his den. Five strides into his journey, he looks up and sees 30 horned sheep blocking his way. There is no mistaking the meaning behind their level stares. It is clear he will not be allowed to leave until the shepherd returns. He is hungry, but it is also clear he will not sup on sheep. His hunger is assuaged by the rams' proffered selection of snakes and field mice, which he quickly wolfs down. While he eats he resigns himself to the notion of being protector of the sheep for the next few days, though he thinks they could well fend for themselves.

On the third day the shepherd returns as promised, but travels only as close as he must in order to see and count the sheep. He has no desire to confront the immense wolf again. Satisfied the sheep number is the same as when he left them three days ago, he takes his leave to start a new and, he hopes, exciting life at sea. He bids the sheep and the wolf a silent farewell.

The wolf spots the far-off shepherd and, seeing he comes no closer, decides a blast from the alp horn is warranted. He wishes fervently to tell the shepherd to take back his flock; that the danger from wolves is no longer a concern.

However, search as he might, the horn is not to be found. That the wily yellow-eyed sheep have hidden it is all too evident when the wolf looks into their amused eyes. He turns and gazes dejectedly at the shepherd's retreating back.

Months pass with the black-gray enduring his role as shepherd. All is peaceful until the day of the first full moon of the lunar New Year. The black-gray is on sentry duty as usual, when a chorus of howls shreds the night's silence. Bewildered, but on guard, he quickly scans the flock and finds the full one hundred yellow-eyed rams absent. There is again a chorus of howls, and the black-gray bolts towards the sound. Three hills he crosses, and on the crest of the fourth he jolts to a halt. In the valley below him are a hundred rams howling at the moon. He watches utterly perplexed, and is rocked to his core when all one hundred rams turn to him and reveal themselves as the yellow-eyed wolves they have always been.

"How...Why?" breathes the black-gray.

"You are not the only wolf to have had a wizard for a master," says one of the yellow-eyed wolves. "Though your illusion has shortcomings, ours does not. As to why...the twelve wolves you chastised will most likely, with the aid of man, soon join their ancestors. How long would we survive among man if we fatted ourselves on his sheep? Even in our sheep guises man would eventually sniff us out and that would be our end. So we dwell among various flocks and content ourselves with snakes, mice, and the small fur such as man does not overmuch miss. And we are none the worse for it."

"Protectors of sheep," says the black-gray.

"In so much as it does not hinder our longevity, " says the yellow-eyed wolf. "Will you join us?"

A long moment passes before the black-gray gives his answer by way of a bone-vibrating howl at that moon. One hundred throats join in.

Days, months, years, and decades go by until one day, a man, his cloak billowing in the breeze, makes his way to the broad, mountainous pasture. His crinkled, sun-bronzed skin, thickly calloused hands and rolling gait mark him as a seafaring man. And although he has enjoyed three decades of such life, he has never forgotten his youthful days as a shepherd. Indeed, over the years, the nostalgia became all consuming prompting him to bid the briny farewell. Now, shepherd's crook in hand and face set with resolve, he intends to reclaim his flock. It has occurred to him his flock may be no more, having been left without a shepherd for thirty years. Even so, he is crestfallen when his sheep, search where he might, are nowhere to be found. He does, however, come across his alp horn, half-concealed in a crevice and generously studded with lichen.

Retrieving the horn, he cleans its mouthpiece as best he can and blows into the instrument. Not a sound. Five more lung-deflating attempts go through the long horn without generating a note. He sighs. He has been too long away from the horn. Pressing the mouthpiece to his temple, he closes his eyes and concentrates. When he finally puts the instrument to his mouth, lungs and lips coordinate to produce a long, mournful note that echoes across the landscape. He smiles in satisfaction and employs the horn two more times before scanning his surroundings and finding them unchanged. He seats himself and the hours pass, each punctuated at its end by three blasts from the horn.

This he continues until the sun's light fades and a full moon illuminates the land.

Sighing heavily, the man rises to his feet and is about to turn to descend into the village, when distant movement catches his eyes. At first glance it seems as though a great, frothy mass is oozing from the mountain, but further study reveals the truth. Sheep. Hundreds upon hundreds of sheep, having heard the distant notes from the horn, come in answer to the calls.

"So many sheep..." breathes the man in wonder, as they spill onto the pasture. His chest swells and moisture wells around his eyes as old feelings of 'shepherdhood' stir within him. Suddenly, other old feelings rush to the fore. He stiffens, sweat springs from his brow, and the staff creaks under the pressure of his tightening grip. For he realizes a darker body helms the flock.

A huge, black ram backed by nigh one hundred gray rams and countless white sheep lumbers purposefully towards him. Abruptly, the dark leader breaks away from the pack and, dipping its head low, plows into the man. The ram then stands over the sprawled form and red eyes that flare like twin fires bore into those of the man. For a fleeting moment, a mixture of recognition and amusement shines within those flaming orbs. And then the ram bares its teeth and utters in a rich baritone, "Mmmm-baaaa". Having said that, the ram busies itself munching the grass surrounding the shepherd's horizontal form.

When the pain of the salutation subsides, the shepherd slowly and shakily regains his feet. Greatly bemused, he turns over in his mind the events that have just taken place. His greeter is undoubtedly the wolf-ram he left in charge of his flock decades ago; the blazing eyes confirm the fact. Yet, it is changed. The finger-long canine teeth are no more, likewise, it seems, the ram's ability to impart human speech. Turn it over as long as he might, the shepherd will find no answers to the riddles. For how can he fathom the workings of wizards, their spells, and the shortcomings of such spells, which, having run their courses, have left their recipients as bona fide sheep.

High in the moonlit Alps, the shepherd, wrapped in a woolen cloak against the night's chill, watches over his flock. He shivers slightly and tugs his garment more tightly about him. As he does so he glances at the black, cud-chewing ram situated at his feet where it befogs the air with its mighty exhalations whilst regarding him intently with its luminous, red oculi. The shepherd shivers again and swallows hard. Leaning lightly on his ever-present shepherd's crook, the shepherd reflects upon the life he leads. It is a life into which he was born. And he doubts there is in the entire world a walk of life that is more exciting than his.≡

Glossary

Words often have more than one definition. We have listed only the meaning used in the story. You can learn more ways to use the word by checking a dictionary.

abandons—leaves a place with no intention of returning

abode—home

abruptly—suddenly and unexpectedly

absence—time away; not being present

absolute—used to give strong emphasis to what is being said

absorbed—occupied completely; totally focused on something

absorbs—take something in mentally; learns; understands

abundant—plentiful; present in great quantity

account—to do something in a way that does justice to your abilities or character

ache—want something very much

acknowledge—show awareness of something

acquire—get something

acres—a large amount of land; each acre is 4,840 square yards

administer—be in charge of and manage the affairs of a business

admonishes—rebuke or correct someone mildly but earnestly

advanced—far along; at a point late in the progress of something

adventure—exciting experience

afford—provide or supply something

affrightened—impressed with sudden fear

aflame—in flames; blazing; on fire

aflutter—excited; in a state of agitation

aerate—allow air to circulate in or penetrate something

agitated—made anxious; disturbed

agreement—a state of having made the same decision as someone else

aimlessly—without purpose or direction

alarm(ed)—fear caused by perception of danger

alacrity—promptness; speedy readiness

alley—small street

aloft—high up; in a higher position

alpha male—dominant male animal in a pack

alp horn—a long horn used in the European mountains

Alps—high mountains capped with snow in France, Switzerland, and Italy

alternate—serving as a backup; another way or option

although—in spite of the fact that

amasses—gather together a large amount; collects

amazement—a strong feeling of wonder or surprise

amended—changed; improved; corrected

amusement—feeling something is funny or entertaining

ancestors—distant relation somebody is descended from, especially somebody more distant than a grandparent

ancient—very old

animate—make active or lively

anniversary—a day set aside every year for marking an important event

announces—tells something publicly; say in a forceful, formal way

anticipating—expecting something; to think something will happen

anxious—eager; wanting to do something very much

apartment—a small home in a larger building with other similar units

apologizing—the act of saying you are sorry for something which has upset someone else

apology—a statement of remorse

appetite—desire for food

appetizing—making one hungry

appreciation—gratefulness

apprehensive—fearful; worried something bad will happen

apprentice—somebody being trained by a skilled professional

approaches—moves closer to somebody or something

approvingly—with a favorable opinion of somebody; liking somebody

aquarium—a glass container for keeping fish

arises—to happen or exist as a result of something

army—a large organized group

aroma—a smell, especially a pleasant one

array—a large number of things

arrested—stopped suddenly

ashamed—feeling full of shame

askew—at an angle; off center

assemblage—gathering together of things or people in one place

assemble—bring people or thing together in one place

assess—judge or examine something

assistance—help given to another

assuaged—provided with relief from something distressful or painful

assured—convinced somebody; overcame somebody's doubt

astonished—to be amazed

astonishment—great amazement

atones—make up for a sin or mistake

attention—mental focus, concentration; notice and interest

attentive—careful; with concentration and focus

auto insurance—protection against loss of the auto

avenue—a wide road; way to proceed

average—typical; ordinary

awakens—wakes up from sleeping

awestruck—filled with a feeling of mixed wonder and dread; amazed

awful—very bad or unpleasant

backbreaking—involving enormous physical effort

back yard—a yard behind a house

balance—be steady on a narrow base

bangled—decorated with bangles or bracelets

banish—send somebody away as punishment; exile; get rid of

bargain—pact; an agreement between two people in which each promises to do something for the other

barging in—moving roughly; pushing somebody or something roughly

baritone—a deep voice; a voice in the lower range of sound

bear witness—to tell others about something that one saw or knows

beauteous—beautiful to look at; very pretty to see

beautiful—pleasing to look at

beckons—motions to someone to come nearer with the hand

befogs—covers or hides something from view with fog or mist

befuddlement—confused; not understanding something

behavior—way of acting

beheld—looked at; fixed one's eyes upon

behest—order or request

bejeweled—decorated lavishly with jewels

bellows—1) shouts in a big voice; roars; yells 2) device for pumping air

belongings—things someone owns; personal possessions

bemused—confused; muddled; puzzled

Bermuda shorts—knee-length shorts

beseeches—begs for something; asks urgently

betray—go against a promise

bevy—group of birds, animals or people

bewildered—confused; puzzled; not understanding

bewitched—to be under a magical spell; enchanted

bid(s)—tell(s) or invite(s) someone to do something

bide—to stay, remain, or wait

biding—stays; waiting

Big House—slang for a prison

billowing—moving in a curling or rolling way like waves or smoke

binds—wraps something tightly

bioluminescent—light coming from a animal, insect, or plant

blackboard—board on which to write things with chalk

bleat(s)—complain(s) annoyingly

blurry—fuzzy; unclear

bluster—behave in a threatening way; bullying

boisterous—noisy, energetic, rowdy

bolt—rush away

bona fide—authentic and genuine in nature

booed—expressed disapproval or dissatisfaction

bore—to penetrate into the hidden parts of somebody

bottom—somebody's buttocks

bottomless—very deep; so deep as to appear to have no bottom

bovine—cattle; cow

bowels—deepest or innermost part of something

bowled—rolled over quickly and smoothly

brambles—prickly plants; vines covered in thorns

branded—to be known as being of bad character

brawny—muscular and strong-looking

breaches—makes an opening through something

breadcrumbs—tiny pieces of bread

bridles—show anger or indignation, sometimes by raising the head

brilliance—extreme brightness or radiance

brimstone—sulfer or sulpher (both spellings are correct), a chemical which has the smell of rotten eggs that is found in rocks

briny—sea

bristle—make the hair or fur stand upright in fear or anger

broiled—cooked under direct heat

bruised—hurt; injured

Webb's Wondrous Tales Book 4

bulk—large body, size, or mass

bull—male animal of whales, cattle, moose, seals, and elephants

bunch—gather in a tight group or cluster

buoy—keep something from falling or sinking

burbling—making bubbling noises

business end—the part of a tool that performs the intended function

bustling—busy; full of activity

calloused—having thick hardened skin, usually a result of hard work

canines—1) any of the dog family including wolves, coyotes, and foxes; 2) pointed tooth between the incisors and the first bicuspids. Most mammals have two in each jaw.

capacity—the maximum amount that can be held or taken in

carefully—cautiously; showing close attention to detail; watchful

carnival—outdoor amusement show

cartwheels—acrobatic movements in which the body is turned sideways onto the hands, then over onto the feet again

catalyst—something that makes a change or event happen

cauliflower—a white flower head eaten as a vegetable

cautiously—carefully; slowly

cease—stop something; end; stop happening

celebrate—show happiness about something

celebration—mark a special happy occasion with a ceremony or party

certainty—surely correct; without any doubt

chamber—an enclosed space or cavity

chant—words repeated to the point of monotony

chaos—a state of complete disorder and confusion

character—typical behavior of a particular person

charges—people or animals being taken care of

chastised—punished

cheaply—costing little; low in price

checked—limited; stopped suddenly; halted or slowed

chide—correct someone gently; tell someone off

chopping block—a heavy block of wood for chopping wood

chops—jaws; mouth

chorus—many voices together

chow line—"chow" is slang for food, a chow line is how food is served in a cafeteria with the person being served progressing along a line of servers dishing out food

churn—move unpleasantly; feel unsettled

circlet—decorative band worn on the head

circuit—a regular trip around a route

circumstances—events or occurrences; the way an event happens

clamp(ed) (s)—held (holds) firmly and tightly

clasp—hold firmly; grasp tightly

cloak—something that covers or conceals

cluster—form a tight group

clutched—held something tightly

coaxes—gently make something work

collapse(s) (d)—falls (fell) down suddenly

combs—searches thoroughly

comfortable—making somebody relax

commands—orders; instructs someone to do something

commandingly—with the ability to impress and control

communicate(s)—give information; share a feeling or thought with somebody else so it is clearly understood

companionably—as friends; friendly, sociable, and good company

companions—somebody who shares time with another

competition—contest; process of trying to win or do better than others

complicate—make something more difficult or harder to do

compliment—something said to express praise or approval

compose—to make calm

comprising—to be made up of

concentrates—thinks intensely about something

concludes—decides; judges based on everything then known

concrete—a hard mixture of sand, small stones, and water

condiments—food seasoning used at the table i.e. salt, pepper, mustard

condition—something that must happen first in order for something else to occur

confinement—restriction or limitation to certain boundaries

confirms—proves something to be true

confesses—admits to having done something wrong

confusion—puzzlement; misunderstanding; bewilderment

conjures—performs a magic trick

consciousness—somebody's mind

consider—think carefully

considerable—a large amount

constant—always present; always together

construct—a building

constructs—builds something; makes

consumed—ate

consuming—extremely intense; so intense as to take up all of somebody's attention, time, and energy

consumption—act of eating or drinking

contemplates—thinks; considers carefully

content—happy and satisfied with the way things are

continue(s) (ing)—without stopping; to keep going

contortions—twisted shape or position

contrary—opposite of something

converg(ing)(ed)—becoming the same; gathering into one group

conveyance—a vehicle like a car or truck

conveys—communicates or tells something through a gesture or look

convinced—persuaded somebody to believe something

cookpot—a large metal container for heating food

copper—small coin of low value

copse—a group of trees

core—the central or most important part of something

countryside—farm land

courting—trying to win somebody's love with the goal of marriage

corded—having tensed or well-developed muscles visible as ridges

courtship—the period of time before marriage when a suitor attempts to convince someone to agree to marriage

crest—top of a hill

crestfallen—disappointed

crevice—a narrow crack or opening, especially in rock; fissure

crook-necked—hook-shaped device; a crook is a shepherd's hooked stick used to catch or guide sheep

cruel—merciless; bringing about pain on purpose

crypt—underground room, often used as a burial chamber or a chapel

crystal—a clear colorless mineral, especially quartz

cud—food chewed twice by cows, sheep, and other such animals

culprit—the one who did the bad act; wrongdoer

culture—growing of plants; to grow and nurture plants

curled up—bent in the shape of a ball

curs—mixed-breed dogs; especially those in poor condition

customer—buyer; person who pays money to get something

dale—a broad lowland valley

dampens—deadens; lowers

darkened—to get darker

darts—fast move; a sudden quick movement

dash—quick purposeful movement

daydreaming—thinking pleasant thoughts while awake

decides—makes a choice to do something

decline—politely refuse

decomposing—breaking down

decree—official order issued by a ruler or one in authority

dedicated—devoted with one's whole heart to a goal, cause or job

deed—a legal document that transfers ownership of land

deem—consider to be

defensive—serving to protect; designed to defend

deflating—letting air out

defy—openly resist somebody; refuse to obey a command

dehydrated—needed water

dejected(ly)—feeling sad; very unhappy

delectable—delicious; something very tasty

delicious(ness)—good to eat; having an enjoyable taste

demonstration—display showing how to do something

den—a hidden home for a wild animal

departure—the action of leaving on a journey

descend—to go down a staircase, hill, or other downward slope

descent—trip down ; going down

desperate—as a last resort; done in great need

destination—the place to which somebody is going

deterred—discouraged or prevented from taking a particular action

dethroned—removed a ruler from power

devises—thinks something up

difficult—hard to do

digesting—processing food after a meal

digits—fingers or toes

dilemma—situation with satisfactory choices

din—loud noise of confused sounds

directs—instructs; tells somebody to do something

disagree—not agree; have different ideas or opinions; not match

disappeared—no longer seen; to be gone without explanation

disapprovingly—chide; scold; refuse to approve or agree

Webb's Wondrous Tales Book 4

discovers—finds something after a search

disguise—a costume to hide who someone is

dismay—feeling of hopelessness

disperse—scatter in different directions

displays—makes visible; shows

disrupt—interrupt; disturb; cause something to stop

distasteful—unpleasant; not liked

disturbing—waking someone up

diving suit—clothes made for going underneath the sea

dizzy—unsteady, as if about to lose balance; confused

doffs—rids oneself of; puts aside

doles—gives something sparingly

dominance—power exerted over others; control or command

dons—puts something on

downpour—heavy rainfall

dowry—bride's family's gift to the bridegroom

dozy—drowsy; half asleep; tending to fall asleep

dragon—a mythical creature like a giant scaly lizard with wings

drags—pull somebody or something along with great effort

dread—feeling extremely frightened or worried

dreadful—extremely unpleasant

drenched—soaked; completely wet

dresses—cleans and prepares meat for cooking

drool—saliva dribbling from the mouth

drooping—hanging down; sagging; moving lower

droplets—small drops of liquid

droves—a large number of animals

drum(s) (ming)—1) making a tapping sound; 2) attracting attention for something

dual—having two parts

ducking—moving quickly

dully—without intensity; with little brightness

dwells—reside; to live in a particular place

dwelling—house or other building in which people live

earnestly—do something with deep sincerity or conviction

earshot—distance within which sound can be heard

earthworm—a worm that burrows in the soil

efforts—attempts to do something

elated—very happy and excited

elongated—long and narrow or slender

eluding—escaping or avoiding

embers—small pieces of burning material from a fire

emeralds—green gemstones

emerge(s) (nce)—come(s) (ing) out from behind or inside of something

emits—produces something, in this case, a smell

employed—worked for money

employer—boss; one who hires others to do work

enabling—providing someone with the means to do something

encounter—unexpected, difficult meeting

endeavor—try hard to do something

enduring—persisting or surviving; patient despite many difficulties

energy—forceful effort; liveliness

engagement—a commitment to attend an event

engulf—swallow something up; surround; overwhelm

enormous—very, very large; a huge amount

ensure—make sure something will happen

enticing—hard to resist; tempting

entrance—way in; a doorway or gate

eons—long periods of years

era—a distinctive period of time

espy(ies)—catch sight of or detect something; see suddenly

establish—start or set up something that is permanent

eternity—a very long time; time without beginning or end

ethic—set of principles; a system of moral standards

eventually—after a long time; in the end

everything—all the items, actions, or facts

evidences—demonstrates or proves something

examines—studies or inspects something in detail

exasperated—made someone angry often by doing something annoying repeatedly

exceptionally—outstanding; well above average; superior; much better

exchanging—giving something and getting something in return

excitement—feeling of lively enjoyment

exclaiming—talking noisily and loudly in excitement

exhale (exhalation)—1) breathe out; 2) the breath that comes out from the lungs

exhausted—so very tired; drained of strength

exiled—banished; sent away as punishment

existence—the state of being real; being present in a particular place

exits—1) leaves; walks out of; departs; 2) ways to leave a space

expectantly—waiting for something exciting, interesting, or enjoyable

expelling—pushing out with force

experimental—testing something

expired—dead

exquisite—very beautiful; perfect and delightful

extending—offering; to move something toward another

extent—degree to which something applies

extenuating—diminish the seriousness of; providing a mitigating excuse for making a mistake or doing something wrong

extinct—no longer in existence

exudes—releases slowly

facade—the way something appears on the surface, especially when that appearance is meant to deceive

facility—a structure or machine which provides ease in doing something i.e. restroom facilities or transportation facilities

fabled—famous because of being described in old stories

fading—slowly becoming less visible; vanishing; disappearing

faint—not loud

faith—belief or trust, especially without logical proof

fanged—having long, pointed teeth

fare—manage in doing something; to get on in a particular way

farewell—says goodbye; marks an end and goes away

Webb's Wondrous Tales Book 4

farmyard—a yard beside farm buildings

fashion(ed) (s)—made or makes something

fate—outcome; destiny; consequence; final result

fathom—understand, usually something profound or mystifying

fatted—ate to more than is needed

fee—payment for services

feeble—weak

felines—cats

fend—protect; defend

fervently—showing great enthusiasm; passionately; with great feeling

fifteenth—15 times

filthy—extremely or disgustingly dirty

firefly—a beetle that flies at night and gives out light

fireplace—a space in the wall with a chimney for a fire

firewood—wood burned as fuel

fix—a difficult situation

flailing—swinging something around wildly

flaps—flys by moving wings up and down

flares—burn brightly

flatbread—bread in round flat loaves, e.g. pitta, nan, tortillas

fleecy—soft and woolly in appearance

flees—runs away quickly

flexes—bends; moves

flock—group of animals

flogging—to beat an animal with a whip

floorboards—wooden strips of wood that make the floor

flops—sit or lie down heavily; letting the body fall

flourish—to wave something around in a dramatic way

flutters—move by flapping wings quickly

foe—enemy or opponent

fogging—thick mist caused by condensed water vapor

folly—thoughtless or reckless behavior; misguided; error; mistake

foolproof—designed to work properly despite any kind of human error

foraging—searching for food; looking for something to eat

fore—the front of something or something at the front

forefinger—index finger; the finger next to the thumb

foremost—most important; in the first position

foreseen—predicted; to know or expect something before it happens

forfeit—give something up

forgotten—lost the memory of

form—a type of something that has different types

former—previous; the one who came before now

formerly—in the past, but not now

formulate—plan something carefully and in detail

foretold—predicted; told before it happened

fortuitous—happening by lucky chance

fortunate—lucky

fortuneteller—one who predicts the future

forward—in front of

foul—stormy or wet or unpleasant for outdoor activities

fowl—bird; bird kept for eating; the flesh of any edible bird

fragrance—a pleasant sweet smell

frantically—excited, hurried and confused by fear or worry

fraught—full of dangers or difficulties

fricasseed—meat cooked in liquid then thickened with cream

frightened—afraid; scared

friendliness—helpful; on the same side

friendship—shared feelings of trust and affection

frolic(king)—play(ing) lightheartedly; frisk(ing) around

frothy—full of foam; having lots of tiny bubbles

fruitful—successful; producing results

frustration—a feeling of disappointment; upset due to lack of success

fuels—to supply energy start or maintain some action or emotion

fumes—fusses; being angry or upset

furniture—tables and chairs

futile—in vain; having no useful result

gaggle—a group; a flock of geese

gaily-painted—painted in bright colors and happy pictures

gait—manner of walking; a way of walking

gaping—wide open and deep

gasping—say something with a sudden sharp intake of breath

gawk—stare stupidly; watch with wide eyes and no understanding

gaze—look at for a long time; stare at with unwavering attention

generate—produce; create

generating—creating something

generations—multiple stages of descent in a family; the time taken to produce a new generation, in humans held to be about 30 years

generosity—kindness; willingness to help

gentle—kind; mild; using little force

genuinely—sincerely felt; real; not pretended

gesture (ing)—an action to express feelings, intention, or instruction

gigantic—very big; huge

gills—the part of the fish used to breathe

gleam—shine brightly

glee—great delight; joy

gleefully—filled with great joy

glistening—shining from light reflecting from a wet surface

globe—the planet Earth

gloom—murky darkness, especially partial darkness with shadows

glorious—outstanding; so good as to merit praise

gobbles—eat quickly and greedily

goldfish—colorful fish

Goliath—in the Bible, a giant warrior who was killed by David using a stone and a sling

gorge—(noun) narrow, deep canyon

gorges—(verb) eats greedily and to excess

gourd—hard-skinned fruit which can be used as bowl or cup when dried

govern(ing)—control(ing) or direct(ing)

grateful—thankful

gratitude—state of feeling thankful to somebody for doing something

greed—strong desire for more than is needed

greeter—somebody who welcomes another

griffin—a mythical creature with the head and wings of an eagle and the body and tail of a lion

grocery—food

grounded—unable to fly

guffaws—loud laughter

guidance—direction; to show someone the way

grumbling—complaining; gurgling and rumbling noises made by an empty stomach

guise—a false outward appearance

gulps—swallow something fast taking in large amounts

gurgling—making bubbling noises

gusto—hearty enjoyment

hackles—hairs on an animal's neck

hails—calls to somebody to get their attention

hampered—made movement difficult

handcuffs—a pair of connected rings that can be locked about the wrists of a prisoner to keep him from using his hands

hapless—unlucky

happened—did something by chance

happiness—state of pleasure, contentment, and joy

hardly—only with great difficulty

harry—cause distress by repeated attacks

haul—pull or drag something; move something with effort

health—general physical condition

heavily—in a slow, clumsy, or laborious way

heir—somebody who receives property when another person dies

helms—steers; guides; directs

henceforth—from now on; forever after a particular point in time

heralds—sign of what will be; shows what will be coming

heroic—showing great determination; large, extensive effort

hero's—something belonging to a someone much admired or brave

hesitates—acts slowly often because of uncertainty or reluctance

hide—the skin of an animal

high state—very good condition

high time—well past the time when something should have been done

hind—rear; at the back of something

hissed—make an "s" sound to show dislike

hoarse—sounding rough; having a harsh, grating voice

hoists—lifts somebody or something up

holdings—legally owned property like land, houses, stocks or bonds

hollow—an empty space inside of something

horde—large crowd; swarm or pack of animals moving in a group

horizon—place where the earth meets the sky

horizontal—lying down

hostile—unfriendly; against somebody

hourglass—time-measuring device consisting of two transparent bulbs connected by a narrow tube and containing an amount of sand that takes a specific amount of time to flow between the bulbs after it is turned over

hovering—lingering or waiting close by in hesitation about what to do

humanity—the human race considered as a whole

humiliation—loss of dignity; feeling of being lessened in pride

hurriedly—done very quickly because of lack of time

hymenopterous—of ants or any of the insects (e.g. wasp, sawfly) with two pairs of wings and a very small waist that live in socially complex colonies which belong to the Order: *Hymenoptera*

idly—not working or doing anything useful

ignite—catch fire; start to burn

ignore—refuse to notice or pay attention to someone or something

ill-tempered—bad mannered; unkind and unfriendly

illuminates—shines light onto something

illusion—false idea; something that deceives the senses or mind

illusionary—a description of something meant to deceive

imagination—creative part of the mind where ideas are formed

imbedded—fixed into something; solidly placed in something

immediately—right then; at once; without delay

immense—huge; exceedingly large

immobile—without moving; motionless; unable to move; still

impart—tell somebody something; communicate information

impatient—annoyed at being kept waiting

imperial—very grand or majestic; supremely powerful

inability—lack of the ability or means to do something

incantation—set of supposedly magic words

incisors—flat sharp front teeth used for cutting and tearing food

infused—filled with strong emotion

ingredients—items in a recipe

inherit—receive something when someone dies

inferior—not as good as another

innocence—lacking worldly experience; failure to recognize the harmful intentions of others; ignorance of serious consequences

inquires—questions; asks something

insects—small six-legged animals like flies, beetles, and bees

instinctively—prompted by a strong natural impulse done without having instruction

instrument—object used to produce music

insulates—wrap something in order to prevent the passage of heat or cold

intact—not damaged; having all parts

intelligible—understandable; capable of being understood

intense—extreme; strong, great, or extreme in any way that can be felt

intentions—aims; things someone plans to do

interesting—enjoyable because of being exciting; not boring

interjects—interrupt with a comment; break into a conversation

interpose—place between two people or things

interrupted—stopped; causing a break in the flow of something

intervenes—become involved in a situation to prevent a bad outcome

introduce—present somebody to somebody

investigate—to look to see what something is or what has happened

invisible—cannot be seen; hidden

irate—very angry

ire—strong anger

jam—stop something from working; block something up

Webb's Wondrous Tales Book 4

jealousy—the state of being resentfully envious

jingle—a catchy tune or verse used to sell something

jockey—try to gain advantage

jolts—shake or jerk violently and suddenly

jubilant—expressing great delight and joy

juggernaut—a crushing force that is relentlessly destructive, crushing and insensitive

junker—an old car that is not well kept

keen—sharp; very good

kelp—a type of seaweed

kindheartedness—friendly and generous; sympathetic and kind

kits—baby foxes

knowledge—information, facts, ideas, truths, or principles

laden—heavily loaded; carrying; weighted down

lamenting—feeling sorrow; mourning for something

landscape—an expanse of scenery for as far as the eye can see

language—way of talking and expressing what you mean

lantern—a lamp which can be carried around

larder—food supply

lark—small brownish bird noted for its beautiful song

larvae—the worm-shaped form of many insects before they become adults

lay claim—assert one's right of possession of something

lays him to rest—phrase meaning to cause someone to die, usually with regard to illness or injury

lest—in order to prevent something from happening

lethargically—physically slow and mentally dull as a result of drugs, tiredness, or disease

lichen—living mass that grows on rocks and trees; a mixture of fungi and algae

lightning bolt or flash—flash of light in a storm

lightening-fast—extremely quickly; very, very fast

lightheaded—dizzy; feeling faint

limb—a large branch

locate—find

longevity—long life or duration

lopsided—unbalanced; tilted or leaning to one side

loses his water—in this case, Finny needs water to breathe

lounges—sits lazily; passes time in a relaxed way

lout—an awkward stupid fellow who is unpleasant to be around

lumbers—walk heavily and clumsily

luminous—bright; glowing

lunar—relating to the moon

lung—the part of the body that takes in air

lunge—a sudden strong movement forward

maiden—a young unmarried woman

maintenance—work that must be done to keep something in order

majestic—impressive; showing great dignity and grandeur

mane—hair on an animal's neck

master—boss; somebody in control of servants

magnificent—beautiful and impressive

malicious—deliberately bad or harmful; meaning to hurt others

manages—succeeds in doing something that was difficult

mandibles—insect mouthparts used for cutting and biting food

mandrill—large monkey with a beard, mane, and crest

manure—fertilizer made with dung; plant food made from poop

marauding—raiding; roving around carrying out violent acts

marrow—soft tissue in bones; the core or center of the bones

marveling—being amazed or surprised

massive—large in comparison to what is usual; bulky: solid

mate—a partner in marriage

matted—tangled; forming a thick mass

materials—things used to make something

matrimony—marriage ceremony

mayhap—perhaps; indicates something that is possibly true

meager—unsatisfactorily small; scant; inadequate; skimpy; slight

melodious—pleasing to hear; tuneful

memories—ability to retain knowledge

menacingly—threatening; being a source of danger to someone

mentally—relating to the mind

mere—that and nothing more, usually emphasizing smallness

merriment—fun and enjoyment marked by noise and laughter

meteor—rock from space burning up in earth's atmosphere

mewl—cry weakly; whimper

mightily—with much effort; to a great degree

migrate—move from place to place

millennia—thousands of years (plural of millennium)

milling—moving without direction or order

millions—a vary large unspecified number of things

mind-boggling—causing astonishment and confusion of the mind

miniature—smaller version of something; tiny

minuscule—extremely small

miracle—amazing event; an act of God

mired—stuck in mud

mirth—happiness or enjoyment, especially with laughter

misdeeds—wicked acts

misgivings—feelings of doubt

mistakenly—based on incorrect information; wrongly

mistreated—treat somebody badly

modifications—changes; alterations to improve something

moisture—wetness

momentarily—briefly; for a short time

monarch—king; ruler

monger—seller; dealer; one who sells goods for a living

monolithic—large and unchanging; massive

moonlit—brightened by the light from the Moon

mooring—place for tying off a cable or rope in order to secure something like a boat, ship, aircraft, or bridge

morsels—small piece of food

mortgage—money borrowed to buy a house

mosquito—small insects that feed on blood

mound—small hill or pile of objects

mountainous—very large or tall

mounts—climbs something; gets onto something

mournfully—with great sadness

mouthing—moving the lips without making a sound

mouthpiece—the part of a musical instrument that is held to the mouth

multitude—very large number of something

mumble—speak quietly such that others can not hear clearly

muck—sticky dirt or filth

muses—says something in a thoughtful way

muster—summon up strength to do something

musty—smelling old, damp, and stale

mutters—says something quietly, especially in annoyance

muzzle—animal's nose and mouth

mystic—another word for mystical; magic-filled

nabs—grabs; seizes; snatches; takes something suddenly

narrowly—by a small amount or distance

naught—nothing; zero amount

navigating—finding a way through a place

nectar—the sweet liquid that flowering plants produce

nectarines—smooth-skinned peach

negotiable—able to be crossed; can successfully pass over

neighboring—nearby; located close by

nerves—courage; coolness; steadiness

nigh—almost; nearly

nocturnal—occurring at night

nostrils—the openings in the nose used to breathe

notion—idea; concept

nudged—pushed gently; moved something slowly and carefully

numerous—many in number

oath—solemn promise; a pledge to do something

obey—do as told; follow instructions or orders

occasion—a particular time when something happens

occurrence—an event; a happening

octopus—sea creature with eight arms having rows of suckers

oculi—eyes; plural of oculus meaning eye

odious—disgusting

oldster—a person of advanced age

onset—start; the beginning of something

oozing—leaking slowly; moving slowly but steadily

opinion—the personal view somebody takes about an issue

options—choices; courses of action that could be taken

orb—sphere; ball

orchard—an area of land where fruit or nut trees are grown

orphanage—place for children who have no parents to look after them

ostrich—the largest living bird

otherwise—in other ways

out distancing—to move faster and farther than something chasing you

out done—defeated; bettered

outcast—somebody rejected by a group; an outsider

overhang—a rock that projects over something

Webb's Wondrous Tales Book 4

overmuch—to excess; too much

owner—the one to whom something belongs

pace—speed of movement, especially when walking or running

palate—1) sense of taste 2) roof of the mouth

pall—a sad, gloomy feeling

pang—intense emotion; sudden, intense, and usually distressing feeling

pantry—place for storing food

pants—taking short, fast breaths, especially after working hard

parched—dry; very thirsty; lacking moisture

parlor—a living room set aside for entertaining guests

particular—fussy; demanding high standards

passage—hallway; path enclosed on both sides

passersby—somebody who happens to be going past a place

passing—death; ceasing to exist

pastured—kept on land with grass for cows

pathetic—pitiful; wretched; sad; skimpy

patient—able to endure waiting calmly

patrons—regular customers

paying attention—listening carefully

payment—reward for something given

peak—highest point

peck—take small bits of food using a beak

peddling—selling goods, especially when traveling from place to place

peels—removes an outer layer of something

pell-mell—in disorderly rush; messily; in a confused, jumbled way

perch—a place or position that is advantageous or prominent

perfection—the quality of something being as good as it can possibly be

performer—someone who acts or sings or plays an instrument for an audience

perky—lively and cheerful; energetic

permission—agreement to allow something to happen or be done

perplexed—puzzled; confused; does not understand

perseveres—persists in doing something despite set backs

pervades—spreads through

physically—of the body; relating to somebody's body

pines—longs or yearns for something; wants something very much

pins—holds down; keeps somebody from moving

pitiful—arousing pity or compassion

plastic—a man-made material which can be molded into shapes

platters—large flat serving dishes for food

playground—play area for children

pleads—begs earnestly

pleasantries—polite remarks; agreeable talk

plight—bad situation; dangerous or unfortunate condition

plopping—dropping with a sound like something flat falling on water

plows—pushes hard and clears something away

pluck—to pull out feathers

plump—having a pleasing amount of flesh

polite—well-mannered; showing common courtesy

pollen—a powdery substance produced by plants

Webb's Wondrous Tales Book 4

portion—a part of a larger whole

portions out—divides among; gives parts of something

position—situation; a particular set of circumstances

possession—ownership

posturing—acting in a way in an attempt to impress or deceive

pounces—move very quickly to grab something

poverty—state of being poor; not having enough money to live

powdery—loose dry particles

practices—repeat something in order to get better

practicing—pursuing a particular activity such as a profession, way of life, or religion

precedes—come or go before something

predictions—saying something will happen before it actually does

preparation—working to make something ready

presence—existence in place; state of being somewhere

prevail—be stronger than; win

prevents—stops something from happening

previously—at an earlier time

prickles—tingling or stinging feeling

pride—group of lions

probes—investigates; checks something out

process—series of actions

produce—fruits and vegetables

professed—declared openly; a publicly made statement

proffer(ing) (ed)—holding (held) something out to somebody

profit—money made from selling something

progress—movement forward or onward

promising—likely to turn out well or be successful

promptly—done right away; quickly acted on

propels—causes somebody to do something; pushes into action

proposition—an idea or plan put forward for consideration

propping—supporting; holding something in place

prospect(s)—the chance of something happening soon

prospective—likely to be something

prostrate—weak or helpless

protector—somebody who defends others

protrude—stick out; jut out from the surroundings

provisions—food and other supplies necessary for a journey

pucker—gather the skin around the lips in such a way that wrinkles or creases are formed

pudgy—short and overweight

punctuated—done to stress or mark something to give it importance

pungent—strong smelling

purchased—paid for; bought

purposefully—determined; having a goal or definite aim

pursuers—chasers who intend to catch somebody

putrid—rotting and giving off a foul smell

quail—a small bird

quake(s) (ing)—tremble(s) (ing) with fear; shake(s) (ing)

quest—search for something, especially a long or difficult one

Webb's Wondrous Tales Book 4

quivering—shaking rapidly with small movements; trembling

racket—loud noise that disturbs people

radiant—showing energy or good health in a pleasing way

raiding—taking something secretly

ramming—striking with great force; colliding with on purpose

ramshackle—badly built or rundown; seeming likely to fall apart

rank and file—in this case it is a description of way the animals are arranged, from the military where troops stand next to each other (rank) and in a line (file) when marching

rations—limited amount of food

raucous—unpleasantly loud; noisy

ravenously—extremely hungry

reality—actual; exists for real; not imaginary or made up

realm—kingdom; a country ruled by a monarch

recall—remember something

recipes—instructions for making food

recipients—somebody who receives something

reclines—leans back into a sloping position in order to relax or rest

recognition—the act of identifying something based on having seen it before

recognize—to know something as a result of having seen it before

recoil—pull away quickly with alarm or horror

recompense—reward; repayment

recovery—return to health

redouble—increase something a lot

reflect—think seriously and carefully

reflection—image that appears in a mirror or other shiny surface

regain—get something back

regret—feel sorry for something previously done

rehydrate—restore water levels in somebody's body

reigned—controlled or influenced; held the royal title of king or queen

rekindles—renews; revive an interest in something

relationship—connection between two or more people or things

release—let something go

relentless—intense and without stopping

relinquish—abandon something; give something up

relish—enjoy something; take pleasure in an experience

reluctant—not eager; feeling no willingness to do something

remainder—part of something left after other parts are gone

remembrance—the act of remembering people or an event

repeatedly—again and again

replacements—something that substitutes for another

replicates—copy something; do something again exactly

request—the act of asking politely

resembles—be similar in appearance; looks like

resigns—reluctantly accepts something

resonate—echo; travel beyond the starting point

resourceful—good at solving problems

respectable—large enough

resume—continue something after a temporary halt

retrace—follow the same path again

Webb's Wondrous Tales Book 4

reveals—makes something visible that was hidden

revenge—punish somebody who harmed you or a friend

reviews—reports on the quality of a performance or product

rhyme—a poem with similar sounds at the ends of the lines

riddles—puzzling or confusing things

rival—to equal or surpass somebody or something

roamed—walk around without purpose; wander aimlessly

rocks—upsets, disturbs, or shocks somebody

rodents—small animals with large front teeth including rats and mice

root—the part of a plant that grows in the ground

rotted—broken down; damaged

rotund—having a round shape

round on—turn against someone

rouses—wakes; stirs into action

rumble—a deep rolling sound

ruminations—think something over carefully; mull something over

rummaging—searching through things

sacred—worthy of worship and respect

sacrificed—gave up something of value to help someone else

sags—hangs down; droops

salivating—drooling; longing for something

salutation—act of greeting someone; expression of recognition

salvation—means of saving somebody from harm or failure

sanctuary—safe place

sanctum—sacred inner place; a quiet private place

sandpaper—strong paper covered with sand used for smoothing

satchel—a small bag for carrying things

sate—completely satisfy somebody's hunger; provide plenty of food

satisfaction—happiness caused by the way something turned out

satisfy—fulfill a need

saucepot—a pot with two handles and a close-fitting lid

saunters—stroll; walk at an easy unhurried pace

sausage—a tube filled with finely chopped and seasoned meat

savanna—grassy plain; a flat grassland sometimes with scattered trees

savoring—enjoying something unhurriedly; relishing the taste of

savory—acceptable

scales—bony plates that cover a fish

Scandinavia—the northern European countries of Norway, Sweden, and Denmark

scans—look around or through something quickly

scattering—throwing things so they land all over the place

scent—smell of something

scepter—a rod or wand used as a sign of a ruler's authority

scissors—instruments for cutting something

scoffs—not believing; expressing scorn

scrumptious—very pleasing, especially to taste; delicious to eat

seafaring—regularly working at sea; a sailor's way of life

seasoned—causing something to become more fit for its purpose

secreting—hiding something; conceal something

seer—one who foretells the future

Webb's Wondrous Tales Book 4

sensations—physical feelings

sentry—lookout or guard

severed—cut through or off

shaggy—long, tangled hair or fur; coarse, uneven hair

shambles—walks with a slow, awkward, shuffling gait

shame—feeling of dishonor, unworthiness, and embarrassment

shave—reduce time slightly

sheer—used to emphasize the unlimited extent or quality of something

sheeting—falling thickly so as to make it hard to see

shelter—a building that provides protection from the weather

shimmers—flickering or wavering light

shortcoming—a failure or flaw in something or someone

shortcut—a more direct way to get from one place to another

shotgun—a gun that shoots small pellets

shower—a sudden spray or fall of something like rain or sparks

showstopper—something so striking it stops the action; performance that receives so much applause that the show is interrupted

shuffling—walk without lifting the feet; dragging the feet

sibling—brother or sister

sifted—separated out from; selected from a larger group of things

signaling—an action or gesture or sign used to communicate

silence—no noise; quietness

silhouette—something lit in such a way as to appear dark, but surrounded by light

simian—of monkey or apes

sinews—strength; power; the tough fibrous tissue connecting bone to muscle

singsong—with a repeatedly rising and falling sound

situated—located; positioned

situation—the way things are at this time; current condition

sizzling—very hot

skeletal—consisting of the bones of an animal

skewered—fixed on a thin metal or wooden rod for cooking

slack—hanging loosely

slaughter—killing of animals for their meat

slavering—with drool dripping from their mouths

slime—slippery liquid, especially one that is unpleasant to touch

slinking—moving quietly and secretly

slippery—hard to hold

slogging—walking with great effort; plod

slumps—collapses; sinks or falls suddenly and heavily

smacks—press the lips together and then open them with a pop

smirking—smile expressing feelings of self-satisfaction and superiority

smoldering—burning slowly; holding in strong emotions

snarls—say something angrily; growl threateningly

sneaks—moves around secretly without being noticed

sniffs—a quick breathing in through the nose in order to smell something

snoozing—sleeping; napping

snuffling—breathing noisily through a partially blocked nose

soars—increase rapidly; rise to a higher level

Webb's Wondrous Tales Book 4

sodden—soaked; extremely wet

sour—turn bad; become worse

sourly—with sharpness or tartness

souvenir—a reminder; something kept to remember an event

sovereign—monarch; ruler; king or queen

spare—an extra wheel kept ready to replace a wheel that breaks

spared—did not harm or kill somebody

spectacle—lavish display; impressive performance

spectacular—impressive or dramatic to look at

spectral—ghostly

speculation—an answer based on few facts

speechless—unable to say anything

spill—flow into a space in large numbers

spirit—enthusiasm and energy

spit—a thin rod that holds meat over a fire

splayed—spread wide and outward

spoke—line from the center of a circle to the outer edge

sprawled—sat or lay awkwardly; with arms and legs in all directions

sprints—short swift run

squeezing—pressing something from two sides; applying pressure

stalking—sneaking up on something or someone

stammers—speaks with hesitation due to strong emotion

staring—looking directly at someone for a long time

starved—suffering from lack of food; extremely hungry

stinging—causing sharp pain, usually for a short period of time

stocky—short and broad with a strong-looking build

stony—expressing no emotion, especially no friendliness or pity

stoops—bend the body forward and downward

stout—thick and strong

straining—making an extreme effort

strapping—tall and powerfully built; big and strong

stray—lost; homeless; wandering; separated

streaked—thin stripe of a different color from its background

strews—scatter something, especially carelessly or untidily

strikingly—noticeable; attracting attention

strides—walk with long steps, briskly and with energy

strolls—walks without hurry, especially for enjoyment

structure—building; something built from many different parts

stuffing—shoving something into a small space

stumbled—walked unsteadily

stunned—made unconscious for a short time; knocked out by a blow

stupefied—amazed; made unable to think clearly

submerged—under the surface of water

submissively—giving in to the demands of another

subsequent—later in time or order

subsides—drops to a lower level; diminishes in intensity

sufficient(ly)—enough; as much as is needed

suitor—a man trying to convince a woman to marry him

suit yourself—have it your way; please yourself

sulking—bad–tempered silence; refusing to talk as a show of anger

Webb's Wondrous Tales Book 4

sup—eat the evening meal

superior—higher in quality; better than others

sun-bronzed—browned by the sun; sun tanned

surf—the lines of foamy waves that break on a seashore

surly—bad-tempered; unfriendly; rude

surprised—amazed; felt wonderment due to an unexpected event

surrounded—to be with; being close to; to have all around one

surroundings—the area right around someone or something

surveys—looks around carefully to consider something

survival—staying alive; remaining in existence

survived—lived through a life-threatening experience

suspicion—feeling or believing that something is wrong

suspicious—thinks things may not be the way they look; doubts

sustained—affected by an injury

sustenance—food

swamp—area of land that is always wet and overgrown with plants

sways—swings back and forth

sweat—moisture on the skin as a result of hard work

sweetheart—a boyfriend or girlfriend; somebody cherished and loved

swigs—drinks in large gulps

swirl(s) (ing)—turn(s) (ing) in a circle

switch—exchange two things; put one in the place of the other

swoons—fall in a faint; sudden and brief loss of consciousness

swoop—descending quickly and suddenly

tainted—spoiled; rotten

takings—money received from sales by a business

taloned—having hooked claws

tangle—twisted together in a tumbled mass

tankards—large heavy mugs

tastiness—having a pleasant flavor

theatrically—full or false or exaggerated emotion; speak dramatically

tedious—boring because of being long

teetering—about to fall down

tended—cared for

test–driving—driving a vehicle for the purpose of proving something's worth

tether—to tie animals with a rope or chain

thin-flanked—have very little body fat; slim

thirstier—needing water more than before

thoroughly—to the fullest extent; as much as possible

thoughtfully—with careful consideration

thousands—a very large number or amount

thrashed—beat; hit hard

thrice—three times

throng—a large crowd of people

thrown—sent something through the air

time-consuming—takes a long time to do

timepiece—watch or clock

toil—hard work

tolerate—permit something; allow something to happen

topples—falls or tips over

totaled—when a vehicle is no longer worth anything due to damage from an accident

totter—walk unsteadily; wobble

touts—praises something; tells of the goodness of something

tow—act of pulling something along

traipse—wander without purpose; walk around

tranquility—peacefulness; free from disturbance

transformed—changed completely for the better

trash can—a garbage container

treacherous—betraying somebody's trust and faith

treasure—jewels and precious objects; something of great value

tree-filtered—in this case, tree leaves block some of the sunlight

trek—make a long, hard trip; travel especially by walking

trepidation—fear or uneasiness

tricks—act of magic designed to puzzle or entertain

tubers—fleshy underground part of plants e.g. potatoes

trudges—walks wearily with slow, heavy steps

trumpet—make an elephant's high-pitched, penetrating call

trunk—the nose of an elephant

tumbling—rolling over

tunnel—a passage through or under something

twice—two times

twinkle—bright unsteady light especially from a small or distant source

unbearable—difficult, unpleasant, or impossible to tolerate or bear

unbeknownst—not known by someone

unbridled—without restraint; openly expressed

uncustomary—unusual; not the ordinary way of behaving

undeniable—beyond question; true or real and beyond dispute

understands—knows the meaning of

uneventful—with nothing remarkable or important happening

unfathomable—too deep to be understood; very mysterious

unforgivable—so bad as to be impossible to forgive

unfortunate—unlucky; involving a bad event

unimpressed—not favorably impressed or pleased

unintended—not the planned outcome

universal—used or understood by everybody

unknown—not known; not part of someone's knowledge

unlawful—not within the law or rules

unlikely—not likely to occur; improbable

unmarried—not yet married; not joined in marriage to another person

unmindful—without attention to; not bothering about

unparalleled—having no equal; not matched in quality

unpleasant—not enjoyable or agreeable

unruly—wild; difficult to control

unsatisfying—does not meet the need or requirement

unspoken—not talked about, although thought about

unsuccessful—not resulting in success; not achieving the intended goal

unwarranted—not justified or deserved

uselessly—not able to be used; not doing what something is suppose to do

utterly—completely; extremely

utters—says something

valiantly—bravely; done courageously but often ending in failure

vanish(ed)—go (went) away; disappear(ed) suddenly

various—many different; assorted

vegetables—plants with parts that can safely be eaten

ventur(es)(ing)—make a trip that is unpleasant or dangerous; risky task

versed—being very knowledgeable about; understanding something

versions—a form or variety that is different from the original

vibrat(es)(ing)—shak(es)(ing) back and forth rapidly in small movements

victims—those hurt or killed, especially in a crime, accident, or disaster

vineyard—place where grapes are grown

visit—to see and spend time with somebody as a guest

void—not containing anything; empty

vows—solemn promises; pledges to behave in a given way

vying—competing for something

waddling—walking with short steps while tilting from side to side

wagon—a rectangular wheeled vehicle for hauling loads pulled by an animal or tractor

warranted—called for; served as a reason to do, believe, or think something

watering hole—place where animals go to drink water

waterproof—made such that water can not enter

wed—got married

weighs—thinks about carefully

weighty—heavy

whimper—cry softly in pain, stress, or fear

whirls—spins around quickly; turns rapidly

wicked—evil; very bad; mean

wiener—same as frankfurter or hot dog

wily—crafty; skilled at using clever tricks to deceive people

winces—makes a pained expression from seeing something unpleasant

wink—shine for a short time

wizened—dried up; looking wrinkled or shriveled

wolfs—eats something greedily and quickly

wonderment—amazement; puzzlement

woodline—a line of trees along the edge of a field

wretched—provoking irritation or anger

wriggle(s) (ing)—twist(s) and turn(s)

wrinkled—lines in the face due to aging

wristwatch—a device for telling time worn on a band on the wrist

writhe—twist or squirm; move in a violent twisting way

yawns—opens mouth wide and takes a deep breath because of tiredness or boredom

yield—give something as a result of work or activity

yon—over there

yowls—cry out mournfully or as an expression of pain; howl

zooming—moving speedily; going very quickly

Meet the author

Mack finds inspiration for his stories everywhere and carries a notebook and pen to record them. He is a graduate of the University of Maryland and a world traveler who enjoys learning new things. His other passions include weightlifting, music, and the large organic garden he tends with his wife, Celia.

Meet the illustrator

Celia loves creating beauty of all kinds. She is an award-winning photographer, a book illustrator, and multimedia artist. She also writes extensively on developing language-related skills. Celia earned a degree in Business from Indiana University, Bloomington, Indiana and in Systems Engineering from the Naval Postgraduate School, Monterey, California. A renaissance woman, she is a co-inventor of a patented antenna design. Celia served 21 years as an officer in the U.S. Army. She now enjoys gardening and creating books with her husband, Mack.

Thank you for reading this Pilinut Press book. We hope you enjoyed it!

We support our readers and educators. Our website has free lesson plans based on our books, book club support including an "Ask the Author" service, interviews with the author and illustrators, articles on developing language skills, and much more. Visit us today.

www.pilinutpress.com

Other Titles:

Can You Keep a Secret?
Danny and the Detention Demons
Little Bianca
The Snickerdoodle Mystery
Webb's Wondrous Tales Book 1
Webb's Wondrous Tales Book 2
Webb's Wondrous Tales Book 3

Feed Your Family of Four for $4 a Day
Publish Today!
Seoul-Full Letters
Small Gym Big Workouts
Finding the Family: The Coleman-Webb-Looney-Phillips
Family History
Mack H. Webb, Jr. Gospel Songbook Vol. 1

www.ingramcontent.com/pod-product-compliance
Lightning Source LLC
Chambersburg PA
CBHW070023260626
47159CB00005B/1932